Tel-talk

art interventions in telephone booths

TEL-TALK

art interventions in telephone booths

Library and Archives Canada Cataloguing in Publication

Poletto, Paola, 1969-

Tel.talk : art interventions in telephone booths / Paola Poletto, Liis Toliao, Yvonne Koscielak.

Short stories.
ISBN 978-1-926639-49-9

1. Telephone calls--Fiction. 2. Telephone calls in art.
3. Telephone booths--Fiction. 4. Telephone booths in art.
I. Toliao, Liis, 1978- II. Koscielak, Yvonne, 1983- III. Title.

PS8323.T44P64 2012   C813'.01083558   C2012-903017-1

Design and Production: Liis Toliao and Paola Poletto
Cover image adapted from Gallery by Halley Isaacs and Hai Ho
Printing by Couch House Books

Copyright © 2012 Tightrope Books

All rights reserved by the individual writers, artists and authors who are solely responsible for their content. No part of this work covered by the copyright herein may be reproduced or used in any form or by any means - graphic, electronic, or mechanical, including photocopying, recording, taping, or information storage and retrieval systems without prior permission of the copyright owner.

Produced with the assistance of the Canada Council for the Arts and the Ontario Arts Council.

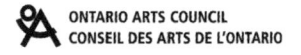

Contents

INTRODUCTION
Tel-talk
.... 555-0009

Directory

Anthea Foyer & Rob King
We Need To Talk 555-0014
Barry Callaghan with Tim Laurin Déjà Vu .. 555-0016
Cathi Bond Night Town 555-0022
Cleen Payphone Therapy 555-0030
Hal Niedzviecki Ossington and Dundas 555-0032
Hayley Isaacs & Hai Ho Gallery 555-0048
Helena Grdadolnik The Case of the
Missing Phone Booth 555-0050
Hitoko Okada Hive 555-0052
Jessica Westhead We Understand Each Other
on a Cellular Level 555-0054
Julie Voyce Flower Arrangements 555-0060
Liis Toliao Hello? Are you still there? 555-0062
Liz Worth Aspirations 555-0064
Otino Corsano Last Call 555-0068
Paola Poletto Lady Cleaner 555-0070
Paul Hong Telephone 555-0072
Ryan Bigge Four Short Calls 555-0078
Sharlene and Paul Rankin
The Telephone Booth 555-0080
Sheila Butler Clark Kent and Superman 555-0082
Stuart Keeler Flagpole (a meta-conversation) ... 555-0084
WeSee Inc. Funbooth 555-0086
Tel-talk Blog Tel-talk.blogspot.ca 555-0088

AFTERWORD

.... 555-0090

Biographies 555-0106
Acknowledgments 555-0114

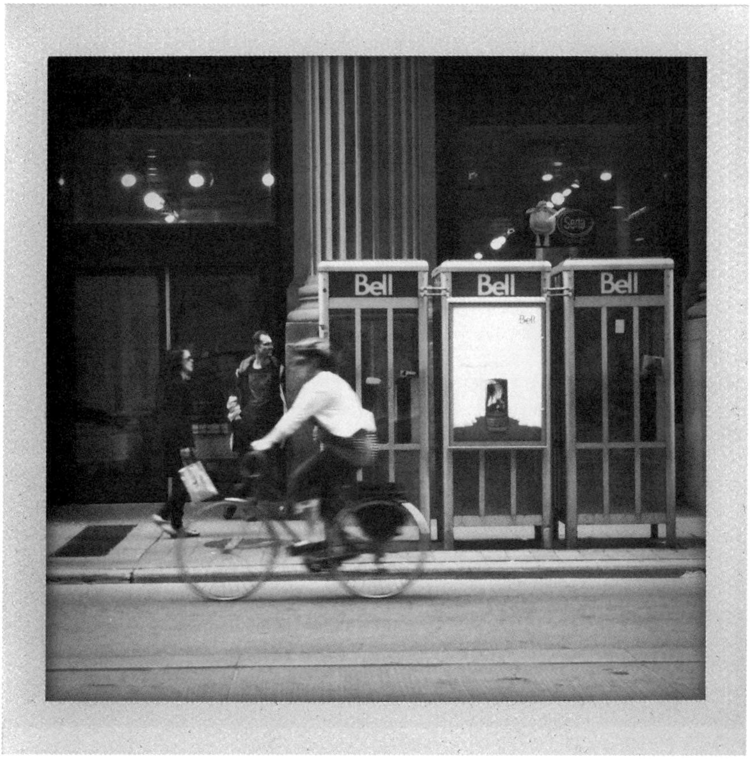
Bell
Bell
Bell

Introduction

The ubiquitous use of personal cell phones in public space has paralleled the slow disappearance of Bell booths at Toronto's prominent street corners. What remains by first account is a smattering of booths near bus stops, gas stations, and high foot traffic zones. When this project was getting its legs, most people responded with questions like, *Who uses telephone booths?* and *What? Telephone booths - they're still around?* There are indeed plenty of telephone booths: in the Greater Toronto Area, over 20,000 of these iconic boxes exist.[1] And plenty of people use telephone booths, either by circumstance or by unapologetic resistance to cells ... or both... and some others use them... to transform into superheroes.

Back in the day, the telephone booth was a great example of our propensity to design a privatized public space. In particular, the Bell booth design stood as an icon for a unified platform for national communication. Today, it still is the symbol of a distinct national-centrist communications agenda, albeit gritty, dirty and street-wise. Many blue panels framed in brushed aluminum over steel frames, encasing a black phone were installed across a vast country - a distinct marriage of form and function. Today they maintain the iconic look but each one also changes slightly from the next. Some have lost much of the blue paneling and are made with long panes of clear acrylic, such as the one located at Yonge and Briar Hill, tucked in the northeast corner of St. Clements Parkette. Others are pedestals for light box ads hanging awkwardly off one side to face car traffic, such as the one located among a triptych of booths at King and Parliament. And others still look more like military bunker boxes, outfitted with 6

Top: Yonge St / Briar Hill Ave
Above: King St W / Spadina Ave

Opposite: King St E / Yonge St

[1] *Gridlock, The week in animosity.* The Grid, Thursday, January 26, 2012.

sides and a strange green cap, such as the ones located on Burnhamthorpe at 427, or on King at Spadina.

What still draws us to the iconic telephone booth is the modular form, its ability to contain the person and give us a defined and perhaps nostalgic, perhaps false, sense of personal space and privacy within the busiest of streets. It also contributes to our delicate if temporal understanding that the democratization of communication is within reach for almost anyone who has 50 cents. Our ability to pay per call is swift and clear and it levels everyone to the same plane. An extensive menu of telephoning options does not complicate the direct call. No long-term plans or contracts, time saving apps or free texting compromising "voice" altogether. There may be a deeper well of opportunities and choices, but our ability to make a call could be really, really, simple… Imagine you didn't carry a personal phone (just imagine!): locating a telephone booth when you need it is *really* hard!

Perhaps our response to the disappearance of the iconic telephone booths - and the fun of potentially transforming the city into a receptacle for very little galleries - is purely an exercise in nostalgia for the booth (someone had recently Tweeted about *Tel-talk*; someone else has responded, *What's a telephone booth?*), and only one of a succession of losses of manned street furniture replaced by such things as instant teller machines, parking meters, mail boxes and newspaper boxes. All of these street furnishings have their roots in services depots with actual people greeting the customer and collecting payment. Even the telephone booth had its beginnings equipped with a heavy door that allowed the attendant to lock the customer into the booth until the completion of the phone call. This prevented the customer from leaving the premises without making payment. And when the customer did leave, we can imagine a slight exchange: a nod of the head, the tip of a hat, the flutter of lashes, or the flip of a neck scarf over the shoulder toward the attendant.

Our assumptions about privacy today are nebulous at best. A scan of folks on any particular bus ride may include a soft romance into a headpiece, where we fill in the conversation's details by the glimmer in the eye, the slight smile, the flushed cheeks. Or we may pay bus fare and witness an incensed monologue about intimate sexual misgivings intended mostly for whoever's on the receiving end… We critique and mental note both the sexual performance and the telephone talker as flat and one-dimensional. No matter. The personal telephone exposes the difference between *the tell* (to tell into the telephone) and *the talk* (to talk in and around the telephone). The tel(l) is for a singular and known audience, and the talk is for everyone else. One is personalized and private, another is impersonal and public, and the experiences are simultaneous.

Tel-talk has brought together artists of varying backgrounds to each perform and/or animate a booth in response to some of these ideas. Artists and writers were asked to consider the relationships between form and function, medium and message, telling and talking… and texting… and more. Specifically, artists and writers were invited to contribute a site-specific installation or short fiction that references a unique telephone booth location. Their work includes a phone call somewhere, somehow… metaphorical or real in homage and out of respect for the beautiful, dirty telephone booth.

The installations began in September 2011 and have continued through to June 2012, and the project has been designed to stay open for the long run. Over this nine-month period, each install was announced as it went up and struck down, and for some, when we learned it went MIA.

The *Tel-talk* project culminates in an exhibition of various works and photo documentations at The Telephone Booth Gallery in Toronto's Junction neighbourhood and gathered in this (phone) book form under the Tightrope Books imprint.

A few people have also gathered their impressions to this project. Helena Grdadolnik looks at the role of informal public art in the city and the many dimensions of public versus private. Ryan Bigge, brings his unfathomable ability to provide a bird's eye view of popular culture trends and drill down to speak about the role of place making in some of the literary contributions to *Tel-talk*. Sharlene and Paul Rankin talk about their nostalgia for the telephone booth and about bringing together gallery art with site-specific art practices.

Everything has clicked - gutsy artists and their art, focused writers with their poems and stories, risk-taking gallery and breakout publisher.

Click - goodbye… no wait, hello…

Hello:

Visit the blog, www.tel-talk.blogspot.com for audio works and new installations and art by Alison Fleming, Charity Miskelly, Don McLeod, Dyan Marie, John Sobol, Laura Peturson, Lizz Aston, Maureen Lynett, Steven Tippin, Tara Cooper and Terry O'Neill, Jake Kennedy and kevin mcpherson eckhoff, TimeandDesire, or to tag your very own intervention.

Paola Poletto, Liis Toliao, Yvonne Koscielak

TALK TO SHUTER ST
CALL:
1 877 509 0077

ANTHEA FOYER & ROB KING

We Need To Talk

..........Bay St. / Richmond St. W. + Shuter St. / Dalhousie St.

Our society is rapidly becoming more and more divided. Right versus Left. Rich versus Poor. Urban versus Suburban. And so on and so on...

We believe that a little conversation, a little understanding, and a little sharing can go a long way. We wanted to give two neighbourhoods a voice with which to engage each other in a long conversation. Specifically, we wanted to connect the financial district crowd with Jarvis and Queen area. At each site we created a warm and cozy environment in each of these phone booths. Passers by were invited to pick up the phone and dial the provided number, where they were greeted by a message recorded in the other phone booth. After listening to the message they were prompted to record a response. This response was then used as the greeting message in the other neighbourhood's phone booth. In this way, one resident at a time provided a voice for their neighbourhood, and created a dialog between the two very different areas.

Top: Booth door, Shuter / Dalhousie
Middle: Inside, Shuter / Dalhousie
Bottom: booth, Cloud Park

Opposite: booth, Cloud Park

Photos by Anthea Foyer

BARRY CALLAGHAN with images by TIM LAURIN
Déjà Vu

..........Queen St. W. / St. Patrick St.

1

I wonder what I'll do now that I have seen the room where I was born in several black-and-white B-movies where there is a south central hotel room some several blocks up from the railroad shunting yards that buffer what was the old lakeshore and there is a single bed in the room, an iron cot against the wall, and on the floor, an old leather suitcase that has been made up into a child's bed, my bed, and outside, there's a hotel sign that flashes on and off, which, after my mother, a brunette with high cheekbones, has gone downstairs to the bar, turns out later in the movie to be the Hotel Rex. The bartender, a retired light-heavyweight boxer who has a moon face and a bent nose, has always favoured my mother for what he says is her beautiful skin. She smiles at him. "Peaches and cream," she says, touching his hand, and then touching her cheek, "peaches and cream. That's how life should be." She smokes a Camel, tapping her ash into a heavy glass ashtray, and she blows a smoke rink and turns on her barstool, crossing her legs, and she says, looking me dead in the eye, "Don't you worry, boy, when the world ends, the world's gonna end on B-flat."

Triptych by Tim Laurin
Phototype on handmade Japanese washi paper

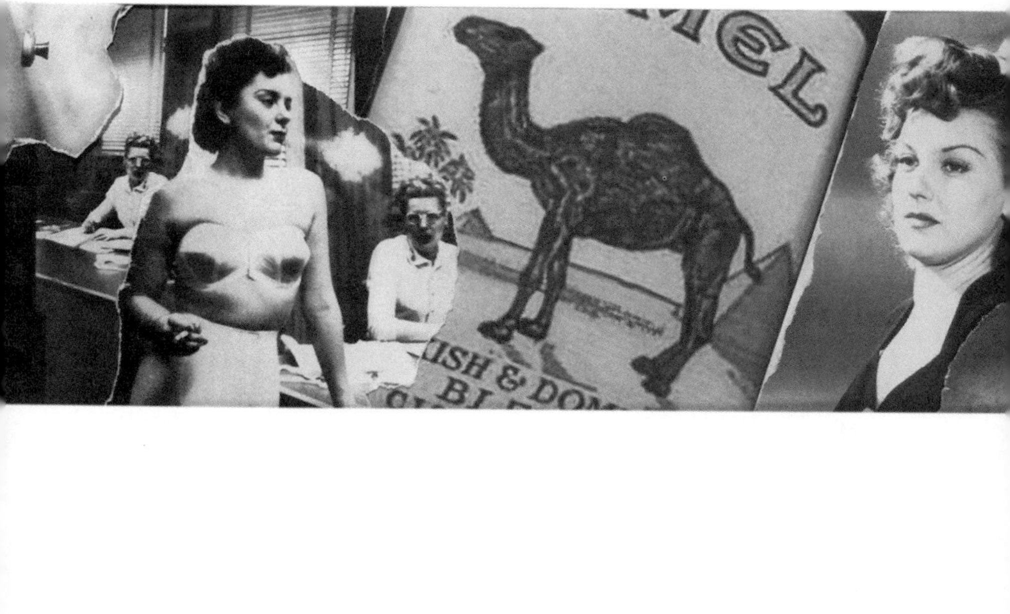

2

She had a habit of falling in love with men in hotel rooms.
In the deadly nightshade hours. She said, snapping a
wooden match head with her thumb and lighting up a
soft-pack Camel, unfiltered, that for each and every lover
(her favourite was a man who sang to her like Larry Parks
singing in the movies like he was Al Jolson singing Mammie
in black face) she always wrote her name for the night
in lipstick on the hotel bathroom mirror: Grace Kelly.
Becoming Grace, my mother said, was actually as close
to despair, to suicide, as she could get. She said she had
countless times tried to kill herself. "But the awful thing is,"
as she blew a smoke ring, and another, smaller, and another,
even smaller but still perfect, "Grace can never die. Not so
long as there is a God."

3

She has called from the hotel. There's a black man seated at a piano at the end of the bar. His hands are folded in his lap. I have seen the piano and the piano player before, perhaps in Casablanca. Somewhere else in the hotel, Illinois Jacquet is playing Embraceable You. Mother has called to wish me a happy birthday. She tells me gaily that I am 43. But she's a day early. Tomorrow is my birthday. And besides, I am 56.

She lights a soft pack Camel cigarette.

At her elbow on the hotel bar is a fish bowl filled with fortune cookies that the bartender has filched over the weeks from an all night chinese Bar-B-Q on Spadina Avenue. Dipping into the bowl, my mother says, "Watch out for how the cookie crumbles," and reads aloud from the slip of fortune paper: Don't reach for the future, let it come to you like a falling tree.

Through parted lips impressed on a window pane she blows me a birthday kiss as Illinois Jacquet appears amidst the smoke rings from her cigarette and the piano player starts playing an old blues called After Hours.

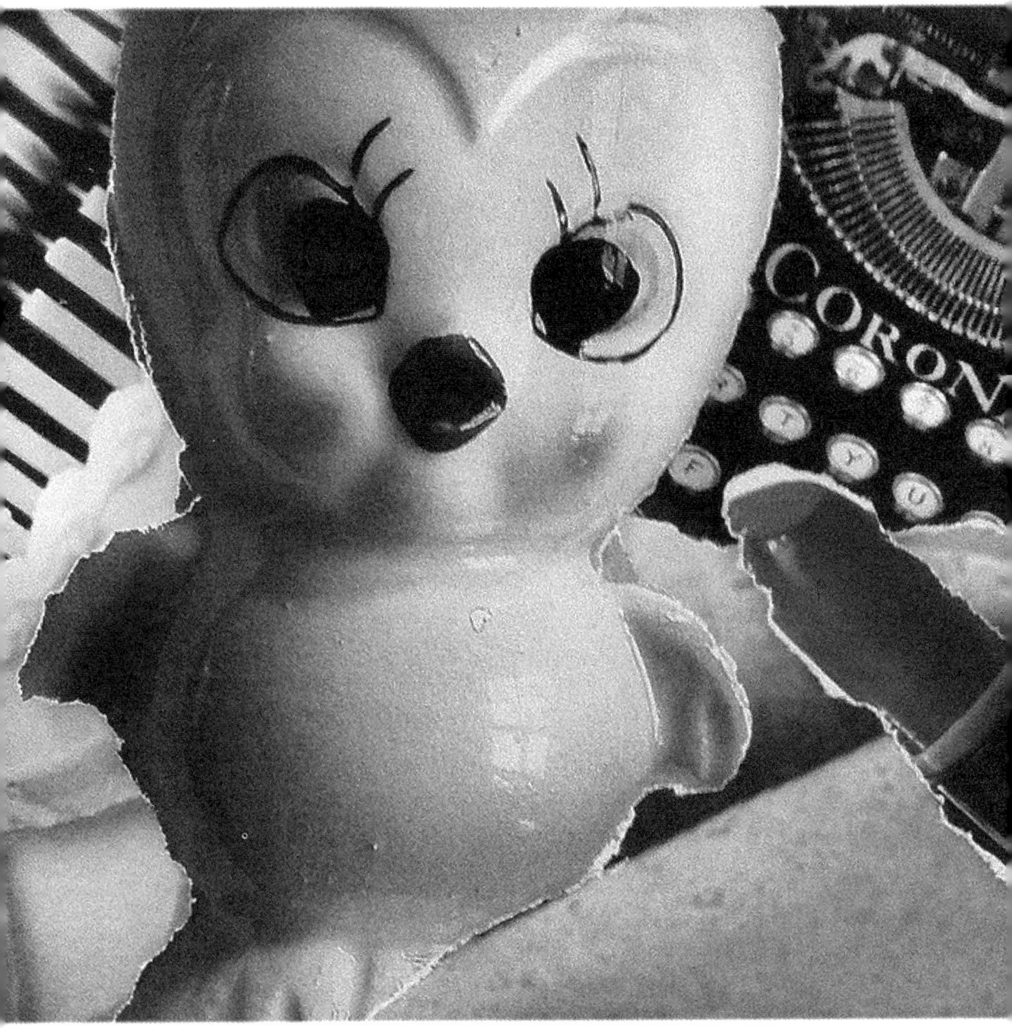
CORON

CATHI BOND

Night Town

..........*Cherry St. / Unwin St. + Gerrard St / Parliament St.*

Unwin Ave / Cherry St

Clarke Beach/Cherry Street Spit was a hang out for drug dealers, users, bikers and cops during the 1970s. A lone phone booth still stands at the corner of Unwin and Cherry, a tactile piece of physical memory from a day when drug deals frequently went down over public phones.

Excerpts from a coming of age novel about the mean streets of Toronto during the 1970s.

There was nothing to do but sit in the back seat of the car waiting for the pay phone to ring. Cope brushed his long, glossy black hair while Charlene nervously painted her nails the same colour as her lips – raspberry. Charlene was Cope's old lady and she wore her clothes so tight you could see the seams in her bra and panties.

I lit another cigarette and stared down the road. Giant oil tanks lined either side of the street. Even though the tanks were abandoned and rusting, I could still make out Shell yellow and BP green. They reminded me of the giant hat boxes Mom kept neatly stacked on the top shelf of her closet. My stomach clenched as I shoved the memory down. When was my brain going to explode? They said it could happen.

The red hull of a giant freighter suddenly floated into view. I got out of the car, running to the water's edge. The seaweed stank. Flapping my arms like a gull, I shouted to the captain, trying to warn him that he was going the wrong way.

But it was too late. The ship was already trapped in the Cherry Beach bay. Dark-haired sailors with shaggy brown hair wearing faded blue caps and matching shirts leaned over the high railing whistling at me. Smiling, I waved back.

Maybe if I got on the boat my brain wouldn't explode, but the boat didn't stop.

Then, like the gulls, the phone screamed. Cope shot out of the car and into the booth, snatching up the receiver. The tails of his long black leather coat were nearly snapped off by the folds in the closing door. All I could make out was "about fucking time!" until the gulls drowned out everything else.

I started skipping around the Cougar. We were going to get high, oh me oh my, as high as the sky. Charlene started waving the red nail polish brush like a wand, telling me to stop drawing attention, but nobody was down here. Nobody but us chickens. The memory stopped my skipping and I got back in the car.

"What's wrong?" Charlene asked, leaning over the back seat.

"Nothing."

That's what Granddad always said when we were playing hide and seek. Mom would wander into the barn calling, "Is there anybody here?"

Granddad and I always hid up in the haymow. "Nobody but us chickens," he'd reply.

Cope kicked open the phone booth door and strode back to the car. He was trying really hard not to be mad. Cope was always copasetic, which is why he got the nickname Cope, but right now Cope was anything but laid back. He got in the car and punched the steering wheel.

Charlene reached for the back of his neck and said "Baby," but he brushed her away. Hurt, Charlene dropped the nail polish wand on the floor and didn't bother to pick it up.

I leaned over the seat. "So?"

"Drought," he replied.

And then we stepped off the edge of an endless chemical run into the nightmare of a full-out crash.

*

We called him Big Man. Everyone was afraid of him, partly because he was way over six feet tall, but mostly because when he was drinking he turned mean. Right now Big Man was hammered, staggering around the parkette at Gerrard and Parliament, having an argument with an invisible enemy, somebody who lived in his mind. The parkette was usually full of winos, but with Big Man on a tear, they'd all disappeared until he calmed down.

I hid in an alley waiting on Charlene who was crammed in the phone booth trying to talk her friend into letting us crash. Ever since Cope got sent up we'd been on the run. Charlene had a green garbage bag in one hand and the receiver in the other. She had everything she owned stuffed into that bag. When I first came to Toronto I had Mom's new monogrammed white Samsonite suitcase, but now I had a garbage bag too.

My forehead was hot. I didn't need a thermometer to know the fever was high. Tilting my head back, I caught the cool water on my cheeks. Steady drizzle threatened to turn into a full out summer storm. There was a loud smash. Big Man had thrown his bottle into the centre of an empty fountain. Fury spent and booze gone, Big Man collapsed on the park bench, flopped over and passed out. Seeing it was safe, Charlene pushed through the pay phone doors, sadly shaking her head. Her friend wouldn't take us in. We had nowhere to go and it was only a question of time before Hermann found me and killed me.

"Maybe Lily will lend me some money," I said. It was my last chance.

Gerrard St / Parliament St.

*

An arcade sign north of Dundas read, "Yonge Street is Fun Street." Lily had taken a job rubbing dirty old men. She said it was better than panhandling. I wasn't too sure about that and Charlene was disgusted. A tall, rickety green staircase led us up to the lounge where a lime neon sign read "The Green Door." Faded pinups of topless girls covered the walls on either side. The red carpet was spotty with stains.

Inside the body rub lounge were sofas, a couple of overstuffed chairs and coffee tables with tin ashtrays and girlie magazines. A sign reading "Rules of the Management" hung over the manager's wicket. The rules were, "No Extras, No Touching the Girls, and Money Up Front." I wondered what extras were.

A pretty girl was lying on the sofa. She lit a cigarette and asked me if I wanted a rub.

"No thank you," I replied, trying not to sound judgmental.

The girl had green hair with matching fingernails and wore ripped black pantyhose, fake black eyelashes and angry swipes of thick black eyeliner. She was stuffed into a bright green bustier and mini skirt.

"Sit," she said and I dropped down beside her, grateful to rest. My brain felt light but my body was heavy.

Charlene remained on her feet, hands on her hips. "Who are you?"

"Helen," the girl replied, blowing a thick plume of smoke in Charlene's direction. Helen's eyes glittered. She wasn't more than eighteen. Helen took my hand and held it.

"You're hot."

I smiled weakly.

"You're scared," she added.

"No I'm not," I lied, yanking my hand away.

"I don't believe you."

There was something kind in Helen's voice. A pudgy guy, probably in his early forties with mousy brown hair appeared in the wicket. He was wearing a short-sleeved shirt with a pocket protector. Leaning across the counter he rubbed his hands and grinned at Charlene. He practically had no lips.

"I'm Ivan. Pleasure to meet such lovely young ladies such as yourselves."

Charlene glowered. I told him we were there to see Lily.

Ivan looked at the clock on the wall. "Should be out any minute. Unless of course things go over," he said, rubbing his hands even harder.

"Are you into glam?" Helen asked.

"What?" I replied.

"Ziggy Stardust and the Spiders from Mars."

"David Bowie's a fag," Charlene said. "The Eagles are a real band that writes real music."

"Your friend's a no taste fat cow," said Helen.

Charlene dropped her bag to the floor. "Listen bitch."

I reached out and touched Helen's bare shoulder to stop her from getting up. I didn't have the strength to stop a fight.

"We just need some money and we'll go," I said.

Her skin was so soft.

While Charlene grumped around the lounge like a Presbyterian Church lady, I tried to change the topic and asked Helen about Ziggy Stardust. Obviously fascinated, Helen sat up straight, crossed her legs and launched into a speech about glam.

"Everyone's either asexual or bisexual."

"What about you?" I asked.

A puff of smoke came out. "I used to be gay, but now I'm asexual. Working here will put you off sex for life."

I looked at Helen. Sure she had green hair, but she was pretty. Was she really gay?

She looked at me, letting out another floating puff of smoke. "You'd be kind of cute if you cleaned yourself up."

The downstairs bell jangled. Ivan poked his head out the wicket. "Sit up straight. Somebody's coming." Footsteps thumped up the steps. "Hurry up," he whispered, scowling at Helen.

Helen repositioned her tits in the bustier, leaned back and posed. A couple of men arrived in the room, looking for a body rub. One smiled eagerly at Charlene.

"Pig," she hissed, snatching up her garbage bag and heading towards the stairs.

I didn't know what to do. I felt too sick to stand, but Lily was still with her customer. I grabbed my bag of clothes and followed Charlene.

"Wait a minute," Ivan said. "If you need a job come back. I can always use new talent and the pay's good."

Helen was still reclining on the sofa but now a man was perched on either side. They were both staring at her tits. She gave me an easy smile, while her boobs powered that room like a nuclear reactor.

We were back out on Yonge Street.

"I can't believe you'd talk to that!" Charlene yelled and then she snapped and started whipping the garbage bag in circles over her head screaming about how Cope broke her heart and everybody fucked her over and she never ever got ahead. That was it. Even if her father beat the shit out of her, she was going home to see her mother. There was no way she was going to whore herself out.

    While Charlene yelled, I sat down on the sidewalk and checked my pulse. It was fast and jumpy and probably came from coming off the speed. The irregularity would eventually pass. After about ten minutes Charlene had worn herself out and she'd come up with another plan.

    "We can stay with my cousin. She won't turn us away. Let's go."

*

It took nearly three hours to get there. We walked west along Dundas through Chinatown's noodle houses, Portuguese bakeries with wedding cakes in the windows, late night cab stands and then wrecking yards full of snarling white-fanged dogs crashing into rusted chain link fences. Charlene kept throwing away pieces of clothing to lighten her load. Every one she discarded was accompanied by some swearing about Cope. I think he gave her everything she owned.

    By the time we reached Bloor we were both ready to drop. Charlene pressed the buzzer. Nobody answered. She pressed it again. Nothing. Charlene didn't have any angry tears left. We hung around waiting until a couple of kids came out, snuck in behind them and took the elevator to the 7th floor and walked down to 717.

    Charlene knocked and softly called out, "It's Charley. Let me in."

    But nobody opened the door. Charlene pulled what was left of her clothing out of the garbage bag and made a pillow for herself on the floor telling me to do the same.

    "We'll just rest our eyes for a bit," Charlene said, dropping onto the carpet. "And then I'm going home. I swear to God I'm going home," she mumbled.

I sat beside her and nearly lay down. I sure wanted to, but I couldn't. If I did I might not get back up. I had to pull myself up, force myself up and keep moving, because there was no way my life was going to end on an apartment hallway floor. I kissed Charlene on the forehead and told her to take care of herself.

"Watch out for Hermann," was the last thing she said before she fell asleep.

*

The subway roared beneath the pavement as I practically crawled into the phone booth at the corner. A nickel was all I had left. Clickety-clack it fell through the mechanism into the coin box and the line came to life. I dialed the number by heart.

"Hello?"

It was so good to hear Aunt Anne's voice.

"Hello?" she asked again.

I swallowed. "It's me."

"Maddy! Are you alright?"

"I'm really sick."

"Where are you?"

"Do you promise you won't call Dad?"

A truck thundered past.

"Do you promise?"

Another subway rumbled beneath me, shaking the phone booth. I could almost hear Aunt Anne thinking.

"Alright. Where are you?"

I looked up at the crossroads. "Dundas and Bloor."

"You stay put. I'll be right there."

The line went dead. I sat down in the phone booth and passed out cold.

Bloor St W / Dundas St W

Looking for some unqualified payphone therapy? Call the Experts at
647-933-9006

TEL-TALK
.BLOGSPOT.COM

24 hour service available from April 1 - 30 2012

cleen

CLEEN

Payphone Therapy

..........*College St. / Crawford St.*

A number to call was provided at the booth. Though we did not invite the callers to leave a message after the scripted messages, we had hoped that some people would.

Choose either your mother or your father. Picked one? Good. Say their name out loud. (Pause) You can say it louder than that. Besides people think you are talking to someone right now, you might as well speak. Say his or her name one more time. Mean it. Now for the hard part. Keep the same parent's name and follow it with one of the these two statements:

        Option 1: --- you fucking let me down.
        Option 2: --- don't fucking leave me.
        (Repeat)

(Excerpt from message script)

HAL NIEDZVIEKI

Ossington and Dundas

..........*Ossington Ave. / Dundas St. W.*

Hello.
Hey. Hi. I was wondering. Is anyone, uh, free, at four?
At four? Let me just see....We've got Dallas, Jenny, and Terri.
Uh, Dallas, is she...
She's 24, 34B, long blonde hair.
Uh...
Did you want to book with her?
I...what's...uh...Terri like?
Terri? Terri's a brunette, she's a 36C, she's 21. She's real fun.
Okay.
Okay, you want to see Terri?
Sure. Yeah.
What's your name?
My name?
I need a name, to make the booking.
Oh, it's, uh, Ian.
Okay Ian, what's your cell number so I can call you back to confirm?
I...uh...I don't have a cell number. I mean, I don't have one you can...I'm calling from a pay phone.
Did you just want to give me a call back about fifteen minutes before four to confirm?
Sure, that would be great.
Okay, that's Terri at four.
Great. Great.

Hey it's Lin.

Lin! Where are you?

I'm at Ossington and Dundas. Where are you guys?

We're just on Ossington, we're walking down Ossington. We're going to this bar, hey, you guys, it's Lin, what's that place called where we're…? Watusi…Yeah we tried to get into that pizza place, Libretto, but it was full so we left our name and then walked down the street to this place for a drink. They're gonna call me when our table is ready in, like, half an hour.

Okay, cool. I'll meet you over there. Watusi?

Yeah, Watusi. It's like, halfway down Ossington. Hey where are you calling from? Your number came up weird.

I know. My cell died. I'm calling from a pay phone.

Oh. They still have those?

I know. It's disgusting in here. There's a drug store on the corner. I'm totally gonna buy some Purell.

Okay, cool. We'll see you over here.

Hey is…

Yes Lin, Tom's here.

Annie!

Should I put him on?

Annie, stop it!

Ohhhh Tommieee…

Annie, I'm serious. Stop it!

See ya in a minute Lin.

Annie, don't say anything!

In a while, crocodile!

Annie!

Dad?

Tara?

I'm…I don't feel good. Can you pick me up?

Tara, where are you?

I'm at the corner of…it's….

Where are you?

Can you pick me up?

Are you *drunk*? No…hold on...it's Tara…I'm trying to…

Dad…

Goddamit Tara. Where are you? Tell me where you are and I'll come and get you.

I'm at the corner…I'm at…

Tara? Where are you? Just walk to the corner and tell me the streets.

I'm…can you just….

Tara? What? I can't hear you? Who's with you?

No no no no. I just…pick me up. Can you just…

Tell me where you are honey. What do the street signs say?

I feel like I might…

Jesus. She's throwing up. Tara are you there? Are you okay? She's drunk. She's pissed drunk. No…I don't know! I can hear somebody. Cyn! Just shut up for a second…Tara! Are you okay honey?

Dad I…I don't feel well.

I'm going to pick you up. Can you see where you are honey? Or ask someone? Is someone with you? Who's with you honey? I hear voices.

I'm on a…I'm on the…pay phone.

A pay phone? She's on a pay phone. I don't know…will you just – Tara, where's your cell?

I…I think I…Dad I….

Jesus!   She's throwing up again. No, she won't tell me. I can't go get her if she doesn't tell me where she is, can I? Just let me…Honey are you there? Are you there hon?

Can you pick me up?

Where are you honey?

Dad?

I'm here baby. Just tell me where you are. Who's with you? Is Billy with you?

I'm just a little, we…we're…I went with Sarah…

Went where? Tara, where are you? Who's Sarah? Is she with you?

Billy…Billy's a fuckin'….Pick me up, I'm…

What? What are you talking about? Who's Sarah? Is she there? She's talking about someone named Sarah. Do you know who this Sarah is?

Can you pick me up now?

Just tell me where you are, honey and I'll come and get you.

We went downtown. Me and…

Downtown! Jesus, Cyn, she's downtown.

Dad?

Honey, can you just tell me where you are? Where are you downtown? Ah…shit. She's…I think she's puking again. Jesus. What a mess. Jesus Christ. Honey? Baby doll? Are you there? Tara?

Is this Pam?

Maybe. Who's this?

Uh. Bob.

Uh huh. Bob. Nice. Are you one of Patrick's buddies?

Who's Patrick.

Whatever. I'm hanging up now.

No. No. Don't hang up.

Whatever, dude. I'm so call blocking you.

No, wait. Let's talk a bit. Just until the bus comes.

The bus?

I'm waiting for the bus. I'm on way to work.

Where do you work?

At the butchers, Nossa Talo.

The one on Dundas?

No, the one on Bloor. I'm on Dundas right now though.

You're on Dundas?

Yeah, Dundas and Ossington. I'm just waiting for the bus.

Are, you're a buddy of Patrick's right? Tell him he's an asshole. Tell him he can fuck off and die.

I'm not a buddy of Patrick's. I don't even know Patrick.

Who are you then?

I'm Eduardo.

Eduardo? I thought you said you were Bob.

I made that up.

Who are you?

I told you, I'm Eduardo.

Okay Eduardo, but who are you?

I'm just a guy. I saw your number. I was waiting for the bus. And I thought. I'll call. While I'm waiting, I'll just call.

What? What are you talking about you saw my number?

On the phone booth here. There's a pay phone here. And someone wrote on the side, on the wall, you know?

What? Wrote what? What the fuck did he do! Tell me what he fucking wrote Eduardo.

He wrote, it says…you know…your name and stuff…

What? What stuff? What the fuck kind of stuff?

It says…For a good time…you know…It says for a good time call…you know?

No I don't fucking know. What a fucking asshole. I'm gonna fucking kill him, you know what I'm talking about Eduardo? I'm going to fucking kill him. Who the fuck does he think he is?

I told you, I don't know him.
So you don't know him? You really don't know him?
I don't know him. I was just waiting for the bus, and I saw, what it said. And I had some change, you know, you get that change in your pocket, I hate that, I hate having all that change jingling around in my pocket, so I put the money in the pay phone and I dialed the number.
You just dialed my number?
Yeah.
You think I'm gonna give you a good time?
No, no, I just…It's just a joke, I'm waiting here for the bus, you know, and I just…I wasn't trying to…
I'll fucking kill him. You see him around you Eduardo you tell him I'm gonna fucking kill him.
I don't even know who he is.
He's an asshole.
He sounds like an asshole.
Believe me, he is. He's a real asshole.
Anyone who would write that about a nice girl, a nice girl like you.
How do you know I'm a nice girl?
You sound like a nice girl.
Do I?
Sure you do, you know. A real nice girl.
So Eduardo, you work at the butchers. You a butcher Eduardo?
Yeah I'm a butcher.
You sound like a nice guy too Eduardo. Are you a nice guy?
Sure, sure I am. I'm a real nice guy. Listen, I gotta, my bus is coming.
Your bus is coming?
Yeah, it's coming.
How about you get the next one?

I gotta go now. The bus is here.
Get the next one, okay Eduardo?

Hello.
Hi. It's…Ian calling. Do you have anybody available at 4?
At four. Let me just check and see who's available…
--
We've got Debbie. We've got May. May's Asian, 32A, 5'1.
She's real cute.
Is…uh…Terri available?
Terri? I think…Terri's free at 5 Ian. Does that work for you?
That's great. That definitely works for me.
Okay, you're booked for five, Ian.

I'm calling from a payphone.
Why a payphone?
It's something different.
Different how?
I don't really know. It's more real
Real?
Cell is so impersonal, you could be anywhere. And calling from home is so boring. Everyone's got those wireless ones now, you're walking around in your dirty sweatpants, you're talking on the phone, you're loading the dishwasher, you're tidying up, I don't know.
Do you have a dishwasher Peter?
What? Sure I do.
Do you load it when we're talking?
No. But I could. That's the point. I could. A pay phone is all about the phone call. You can't do anything. You can't go anywhere. You're in a particular place and time. You're right

there. It's hard to explain. But it feels different.
So where are you?
I'm at the corner of Ossington and Dundas. I went to the liquor store near here. I bought a bottle of wine. A real nice Amarone. Then I saw the payphone. Then I thought of you.
What does it look like?
What?
The corner. Where you are.
Why don't you come find out for yourself?
You know I can't do that Peter. I know you won't.
Peter…please…you're my eyes and ears.
Here. Listen.
--

What did you hear?
I heard traffic. Cars. People. People talking.
There are people here waiting for the bus.
What kinds of people? Describe them.
I don't know. All kinds of people. Just…people.
Tell me about them Peter.
--

Peter…
Alright. Alright. There's a black woman. She's fat. She's got a kid with her, a boy. He's fat too. He's maybe six or something like that. I don't know. I can never tell the ages of kids.
He's wearing a big puffy parka, but you can still tell he's fat. Maybe not that fat. Maybe not like the woman. Maybe just chunky.
Who else is there Peter?
There's a white guy, he looks Portuguese, he's got short hair, he has a leather jacket on and he's pacing. He's antsy. I think maybe he's late for work or something.
How do you know he's Portuguese?
What? I don't know. I just do. I can tell.

How can you tell?
Well there are just…looks, people have, you know?
I don't know Peter.
I know you don't Allan.
Is there anyone else there?
There's a Chinese guy. He's maybe 50 or something like that. He's smoking a cigarette and staring across the street.
What's across the street?
There's a bank across the street Allan. Do you know what a bank is?
Don't be cruel Peter.
I'm sorry Allan. Behind the payphone is a community centre. On the other side of Dundas is a drugstore. It's not a big drugstore like a Shopper's or something. It's a small drugstore. It's got a sign in the window that says "we only supply oxycontin by special order." Kitty corner from the community centre where the phone booth is there's another bank.
There are two banks?
There are two banks. They are across the street from each other.
Is there a line up?
A line up?
In the bank?
I don't know. I can't see that from here. That's what I mean about the payphone. You're rooted where you are. You can't just cross the street and carry on your conversation. You have to stay in place. You're attached.
Do you feel attached Peter?
Why else would I keep calling Allan?
I don't know Peter. Why do you keep calling?
Because I'm your eyes and ears.
What else? What else are you seeing?

People look at you as they walk by. They just glance at you. They're thinking: Where's his cell phone? They're thinking: What's the deal with that guy using the pay phone?
Who's looking at you?
Two girls just walked by. They were 13 or 14 or something like that. They looked at me and then they giggled. They were both holding cell phones and texting their boyfriends at the same time. They've probably never used a payphone in their lives.
Probably not.
Have you ever used a payphone?
Not in a long time Peter.
You should get out more.
Are you going to drink the wine with Raj?
He's coming over tonight. I was going to make dinner but now I think I'll just order in.
So it's a date?
I think we're past that stage. I think we're dong something else now.
What are you doing?
Whatever comes after dating.
Does Raj know you like to call strange men on payphones?
Why? Are you going to tell him?
I wouldn't do that Peter.
I know you wouldn't Allan.
What's happening on the corner now Peter, what's happening at Ossington and Dundas?
Not much, really. It's an ugly corner. Oh here comes the bus. People are getting on the bus.
The fat woman? And the guy who's late for work?
Everyone, Allan. They're all getting on the bus. The bus is ugly too. It's got an advertisement on it for a new movie that looks really terrible. And on the other side it's got an

advertisement for Kelsey's.
What's Kelsey's?
It's a chain restaurant Allan. It isn't very good.
Oh.
The bus is gone now. I'm alone on the corner. Like I said, it's an ugly corner. It's always been an ugly corner. Everything else about this area has changed but this corner hasn't changed much at all.
What do you mean everything's changed?
When I first moved in around here, what?, ten years ago, there wasn't a single decent restaurant. Now I can't even afford the restaurants on Ossington. I was telling Raj this the other night, how there's all new restaurants and bars all down Ossingtoin and spreading to Dundas too. So it's changed a lot, especially on the weekend. But you can't see any of that from this corner. This corner just looks the same as always, ugly.
Maybe that's why people like it?
What do you mean?
People like it because it's still kind of ugly.
I think you're right Allan. If they made it all fancy, the fancy people wouldn't come.
You're right too Peter.
Right about what?
Talking to you on a pay phone. It's different.
How so?
Everything you said before. About being in a place. It's a treat for me. I feel like I'm right there with you.
You could be, if you wanted to.
You know I can't Peter.
I know Allan.
Don't be angry with me.
--

Peter?

I'm not angry with you, Allan.

You're my eyes and ears Peter.

I have to go now Allan.

I love you Peter.

An old lady dressed all in black just walked by me. She gave me the meanest look. Like the evil eye or something.

Oh dear. Do you think she's a witch Peter?

How can I tell?

Quick, make the sign of the cross and eat a clove a garlic.

Just in case.

I'll do that Allan.

You don't have to call me, Peter. If it upsets you.

I'll call you tomorrow Allan.

Peter?

Yes?

Thank you.

It's snowing. I'm in a phone booth but there's a wind and it's blowing the snow in between the cracks of the door. It's a fine snow, gritty, almost like sand. That's because of how cold it is right now, minus twenty, probably, with the wind chill. Isn't that what they always say? *With the wind chill?* I'm the only one around right now. I can't see a single living soul. Not even in a car or a passing streetcar. Jesus, it's like I'm the only person left alive. Armageddon! I guess that's what you get when you wander around at 3am on a freezing cold snowy night. But Christ it's cold! Warmer in here though, in the phone booth. But the wind still gets in through the cracks. And the door doesn't go all the way down. So I can feel the cold on my ankles, on the tops of my feet, on the tips of my toes. I'm lying. I can't actually feel my toes. What am I doing out here? Last person left. Last man standing. Urban cowboy. I'm walking heah! I'm walking heah! You talking to me? You talking to me? I'm mixing my movies. It's like mixing your metaphors. Still, same era. Golden age of the anti establishment Hollywood movie. God damn, that was the time to be in movies, if there was ever a time to be in the movies. I used to think I'd get into acting. Move to LA. Sunny down there, warm all the time, I hear they don't even really have seasons. Just sun and more sun. This freaking cold! Didn't you have a friend who moved to LA to do acting sis? Jenny, Julie, she had that long blonde hair, she was so pretty, what ever happened to her? I think she liked me. I remember one time when mom and dad were away and I had that party and she came and you and her got into mom's peach schnapps, and after, after you passed out, we had a moment. We didn't kiss or anything. Nothing like that. But it was like, she just came and sat next to me on the couch after everyone else had left and you were upstairs passed out and she sat near me, very near me, right next to me, we weren't touching or anything, but she was near me, I could smell her and hear her breathing, that's how close she was. And then we just sat there in the dark together. After a while she got up and she went upstairs. Didn't say a word. Neither of us did. God, she was a pretty one wasn't she? Jenny. Julie? Remember her sis? Anyway, I thought I'd get into it, acting, but I guess I got a bit…waylaid. Yeah. You could call it that. The opposite of getting laid. Getting waylaid. Still, maybe they'll make a movie about me one day. Why not? They made one about Ritzo Ratzo I'm walking heah so why not me? I could be Toronto's Urban Cowboy. Found dead, frozen to death in a payphone, but who was he? What happened to him? Let's retrace his steps, god, what a story, this has real potential, tragedy, pathos, everything. Well not everything. A few things missing. A love interest. No problem. Remember Julie? We can just…bump her up a bit. Right sis? A little creative license for the purposes of bringing my tragic story to the big screen. Ah, shit, it's cold. Don't worry. I'm not going to die. Not tonight, anyway. I'm feeling good! Partipaction action! Remember that sis? I'm jumping up and down. Jumping jacks in a phone booth. Just enough room to jump but not quite enough room to jack. You know what I mean sis? Get the blood flowing baby! Anyway, what were we talking about? Waylaid, way laid, ways to get laid. What kind of thing is that to talk to about with your sister? Hey we're both adults here. But let's move on anyway. Different strokes for different folks. They say maybe 15, 20 centimetres gonna come down tonight. I dunno. That's what I heard. Where does a guy like me hear stuff like that? Talk. Talk on the street. You'd be surprised what people know, what people experience. Like this one guy. He was telling me he used to work in a fish plant up in Alaska. All the way over in Alaska. How did you end up in Hogtown? I asked him. He told me a story like you wouldn't believe. Riding the rails, robbing a gas station, getting beat up and raped buy a couple of cops in Reno. Reno! Forget me, he's the one they should make a movie about. But he's a drunk. He's nothing but an old drunk. Who's gonna make a movie about some old drunk? It's probably all lies. He's probably like me, probably never even left Toronto his whole life practically. Not that I haven't seen some things. And done some things. You'd be surprised sis. You'd be surprised. Shit, it's cold! What's the time? I gotta go. I gotta keep moving. I got people to meet, meetings to meet about, whooo it's cold, cold out there, cold in here, you keeping warm sis? Sure you are. Sure you are. I'm gonna go now. I'm gonna hang up now. Maybe I won't though, you know? Maybe I'll just let the phone dangle down, swinging. Maybe I'll just sit down here in this phone booth and close my eyes for a few minutes. You close your eyes too sis. Close your eyes and I'll close my eyes and we'll still be able to hear each other, right? Hear each other breathing.

Hello.
Hi it's Ian. Is anyone available for 3:30? Maybe Terri?
Terri? She's all booked up Ian. She's booked for the day.
Already?
I'm sorry Ian. But I have Marci and Crystal. Marci's 5'8" 36DD, she's a real spit fire. Crystal's Vietnamese, 5'3" –
Can I book with Terri for tomorrow?
I'm sorry, Terri's not working tomorrow.
When's the next time Terri's available?
Terri isn't available for you Ian. I have Marci or Crystal.
Why isn't Terri available?
Terri doesn't want to see you again Ian.
What? What you do you mean? Why not?
I have Marci for you Ian. Or Crystal.

THIS COMMUNITY
PROTECTED
NEIGHBOURHOOD
WATCH
8AM - 6PM
Bell
Bell

HAYLEY ISAACS & HAI HO

Gallery

..........*Dundas St. W. / Morrow Ave.*

This installation created a three-dimensional gallery setting in situ, surrounding the telephone booth at the corner of Morrow Avenue and Dundas Street West.

While booths are disappearing around the city, we wanted to explore both the booth as a fading marker of place and as an iconic symbol of publicly accessible standards of communication. The project attempts to exhibit the object as well as the specific "place" created by the booth.

Telephone Booth - Morrow Avenue, Dundas Street West November 1991

Bell Canada, Manufactured by Industries Jaro, Quebec

Model J800-S #4800-87851, produced in January 1987 Aluminum, glass, silicon, acrylic, polycarbonate, fluorescent light tubes, stainless steel, copper wire, high-impact resistant polymer, circuit boards.

Originally installed as a commercial venture by Bell Canada, this small architecture establishes the corner of Morrow Avenue and Dundas Street West as a portal for accessible communication.

(Text from installation didactic panel)

Photos by Hayley Isaacs and Hai Ho

HELENA GRDADOLNIK

The Case of the Missing Phone Booth

Tel-talk artist Sheila Butler, in describing Clark Kent's changeroom, calls phone booths "small islands of privacy on busy North American streets." The booths are largely transparent (glass or acrylic panels) and set within public thoroughfares yet, upon entering the nine square feet of space, people act as it they are not visible. Do the layers of tags and scratchiti lend a veneer of privacy? Superman himself wasn't worried about being seen pulling on his tights.

The booths themselves seem to hide in plain view – perhaps a function of both their ubiquity and impending obsolescence. When I first heard about the *Tel-talk* project I couldn't think of a single phone booth located near my house. When I consciously looked for them, I was surprised that I pass three fully-enclosed booths on my five-minute walk to the grocery store. The *Tel-talk* artwork makes us notice and seek out these structures once again. The projects speak to site-specificity in a mobile age (particularly Hal Niedzviecki's short fiction "Ossington and Dundas"), but also turn this notion on its head by having a blog as the predominant way most of us have 'visited' the full gamut of stories and installations.

A hefty dose of nostalgia runs through many of the *Tel-talk* projects, perhaps for a seemingly simpler and less-connected era. The corporation that owns the phone booths isn't always well-loved, but its booths are. Maybe they've earned street cred from their heavy use in film noir. Telephone booths are a sliver of dark alley right in plain view. They seem to invite informal, sometimes illegal, uses - the booths withstand a regular tsunami of vandalism, piss and litter. Many of the *Tel-talk* artists created work that made these ill-treated spaces more inviting through cleaning (Lady Cleaner), decorating (Flower Arrangements), or helping (Payphone Therapy).

Maybe with a little love, a lot of art and some reinvention – like John Locke's pop-up phone booth libraries in New York City – the case of the invisible phone booth can be solved.

HITOKO OKADA

Hive

..........Locke St. / Charleton Ave. (Hamilton, ON)

Busy making hive and home, displaced bees gentrified from natural habitat, occupy a telephone booth at an intersection of urban sprawl. A passer-by stops to make a call at the Hive. Coming from the receiver, the bees can hear: *"Hey honey, I'm home"*.

Photos by Hitoko Okada

TEL-TALK
.blogspot.com

Bell

TEL-TALK
.blogspot.com

JESSICA WESTHEAD
We Understand Each Other On A Cellular Level
Overheard random cellphone monologues as slightly less random dialogue(s)

..........*College St. / University Ave.*

"I have an improvement session booked for Friday. And Chantal told me she's not coming. And I'm like, 'Well, sorry, it's mandatory.' So now I have to go and talk to Jamie and say Chantal doesn't want to attend a mandatory session."

"I have to tell you. She said it's nice you're covering and all, but she told me she didn't think you could do her job while she's off."

"Lots of shit going on at work. A lot of shit. The whole place blew up last week without me. And last week's polling meeting that I scheduled, not everyone showed up to it."

"So then I said to her, 'I'm not holding a grudge, I'm just stating the obvious.'"

"I don't think she thinks, is what I think. You know? It's like, no offense, but there you go."

"I don't think she's more smart than me. She just has the confidence to sound like she's more smart."

"Knowledge isn't my forté. I generally just get the drift of things. I don't know much, but compared to some people, I probably know a lot more."

"I did French immersion in grade five. And everything was in French. History. Geography. All in French. 'Le Canada.' That's how come I don't know anything."

"This lady was reading her kid a book about robots, but it was all out of date. The book was old. And the kid was taking it all in, all this outdated information. He's going to grow up thinking that robots do all these things they don't do anymore."

"Oh my God, our high school is so small! It's like incest!"

"Her whole family is quiet. Lithuanians are really quiet."

"I bet if you started listening to your parents' radio station you'd find out where your dad gets all his jokes."

"They're not going to Thanksgiving at Carol-Ann's. Because the family's crazy. And I got the unrated version of Judy at the anniversary party. She kept interrupting everyone's speeches, and she sat on Tim's lap. The usual."

"So tell me. You're at home? Okay, I need to know something. I need you to tell me. Did Janet get a turkey?"

"I don't like meatball subs. It's not real meat. It's bullshit. You should get the steak kind."

"Do you like me? Because I can't tell."

"This time, this is about me. Before I used to do everything for everybody. Not anymore."

"Sure we have freedom. But also the responsibility to use it wisely. You can do lots of things, but if you don't do them well, forget it."

"But you need to make money. You can't call yourself a businessperson if you're running around losing money. If you go bankrupt, this is not success."

"You don't have any money, right? Or do you? Do you have, like, money, and I'll pay you back after I go see Tiffany? Yeah, I'm going to Tiffany's. I want to give her the opportunity to see me on my birthday."

"Maybe if we won like a lottery, or something. Then I bet things would be better."

"We saw you on TV the other day. You were on there! So did you get paid for that? You must've. No? Ah, well. Front and centre, though!"

"Did you see that video? The one where he's wearing a mask and the mask has horns on it and the horns are on fire and he's going like *this*?"

"So I'm cutting the puppet show from the end because that was the biggest criticism—they said it lagged."

"We're seeing the type of play that makes men and women laugh at their differences. Like how we're different, but we're really the same in a lot of ways. But then not really."

"You know that girl Cindy? She has really long hair but she's with somebody, right?"

"I mean, the other day, I saw Kenny and he was wearing a pink shirt and I was like, 'It looks good on you, man.'"

"She's going to be all tanned, though. That's my weakness."

"Just sucks. I wish he was fun to hang out with. I mean, he's good for, like, the first hour."

"You know, she doesn't need a lot of attention. You could ignore her for a week and she wouldn't mind."

"You know that guy with the helmet, what was he called? Aristedes? From history, whatever."

"I mean, I could see that she's not a petite person, like, bone-wise."

"Well, I'm pretty sure he's developmentally incorrect."

"She has that big chin and her teeth are all like…well, I don't know what to say."

"I don't have to wish that on him. I don't have to wish anything on him, he does it all on his own."

"Somethin' else, man. Somethin' else is all I can say about her."

"He has difficulty emoting, I know that much."

"I don't know about her, she's always too exuberant. Plus she's got sores on her mouth."

"What's wrong with him to be like that? He must be abused. He must call the abused hotline every day."

"Georgia is a fucking liar. Beth asked us, 'Who had fries?' Because they weren't thrown out so there were fruit flies everywhere. And Georgia denied it. Only two people in the office had fries today—you and Georgia. So why would you leave your area to deposit your fry garbage on Georgia's desk? You wouldn't, because that doesn't even make sense. Which brings me back to my original point: Georgia is a liar."

"So I was talking to Barry. Yeah, I know you're not comfortable—I told him. If you don't feel comfortable, I'll protect you. I told the guy. Barry's cool. He'll just come over, we'll shoot the shit. I mean, just trust me. I've known the guy since I was twenty-four. If there was ever anybody you could trust, it would be Barry. He's my best friend. No, he's not going to do that thing he did last time again, I swear."

"Oh my God, you totally just, like, verbalized my total inner dialogue to myself!"

Bell

JULIE VOYCE

Flower Arrangements

..........*Queens Quay E. / Freeland St.*

There was a nagging temptation to make a couple of R.I.P. crosses. Why tempt fate? The two phone booths will still be there, in front of the LBCO: sturdy landline back-ups that ooze accountability. So when that sleek sexy jewel of a mobile conks out, when that thoughtful beau needs to check the wine with their sweetheart- our intrepid phones will be ready, draped in plexi wraps, each one sporting a lovely fascinator.

Photos by Julie Voyce, taken with a disposable camera

LIIS TOLIAO

Hello? Are you still there?

..........*various booths*

Telephones taking pictures of telephones. What a world. And how novel, faux Polaroid. There are plenty of apps for nostalgia.

I had set out to catalogue and take photos of things that no one takes photos of. And why would anyone want to take photos of these anachronistic booths?

A conversation between technologies, between generations. Like calling an aging grandparent on their birthday. *Hello! Happy birthday!* The line goes quiet. *Hello? Are you still there?*

As I continued to document, it started to feel like I was creating mementos of a world that is fading in to the distance. Mementos from the edge of extintion.

Top row: College St / Crawford St,
College St / Markham St

Middle row: Queen St W / Dovercourt Rd,
Roncesvalles Ave / Howard Park Ave

Bottom Row: King St W / Parliament St,
Bathurst St / Lennox St

Bell

PARK
Bell
Bell

MARGIS
PHARMACY

CONVENIENCE
and
TAKE-OUT
ATM
Bell

Bell

LIZ WORTH

Aspirations

.........*King St. W. / Portland St.*

1.

The head hasn't been the same
since
the start of our last story.
Suburban girls on the downtown bus,
Unfortunately bland and
on a quiet crusade.
We kept a tip of hair in the mouth,
dried sharp to
compose colour,
lipstain on a face embroidered.

2.

The party, 7 p.m.,
Prozac powdered, coffee table lined up,
hiding in the bathroom with our drinks when
Judy wanted to kiss me in
20-dollar leather pants and an army jacket.
I was too blemished, hypersensitive to become a
curtain of hair, a crush of ceramic and
creased eyeliner.
Against the tiles climbed a
vocal scraping,
our tailbones hard in the dry bathtub.

3.

Sunday was a wall of sore throat.
Our lips, dried white, lungs serrated from smoke.
Cut-offs and black tank tops, stashed and
tiny in our purses: terminal gravity and a
stark craving dominated,
moved us to slip them on.

4.

Persona amplified at the corner of King and Portland,
still early enough to pretend
the streets were only ours: holy our.
You stretched and caught the sun in
blond hairs low on your belly.
Panting, we let sentiment atrophy,
aspired to lightning.

Detour #1

We ran into R. wearing anorexia and Victorian boots. She'd been to the forest electric, had her pace timed by a rush of tongues.

We knew hers was a deceptive cadence, but we followed anyway through lost time and narcotic fascination.

5.

It was the
transcendental medication that
transformed the afternoon into a
wild eye,
sun a droning high note of heft and tone.
It must have been so obvious that
we were stoned out of our minds,
heads down, contact inconceivable.

Detour #2

I called J. from a payphone,
told him we needed to be
held from going anywhere.
An epidemic of instability was
crawling up your legs but
only I could see those shakes.
It was an inferior scene;
I almost hung up when J. finally said
he'd meet us at the liquor store.
We grabbed a mickey of tequila with
unbearable urgency,
an explosion of tremors.

6.

In an apartment above a smoke shop we were
kindred on the carpet, panting into an
expansion of appetite, head full of
erosion into clean dreaming.
We held our faces to the cool floors,

dry lips chapped and whispering against
white walls that held hearts, eyes of wolves.
I felt close to you then,
in that barren consciousness.

7.

Haggard: we'd become tired husks.
On the way home, I forgot which one of us said:

….

I forgot which one of us said:

….

I forgot which one of us said:

….

                              It hasn't been the same since.

Last.Call

Otino Co

an exhibition and publication about locating the public telephone booth.

Tel.Talk

2012

"Maarika 5 Mixdown", 1 of 3 promo posters for audio movie trailers by Otino Corsano. Original voice recordings were conducted on Mar. 16, 2012, with audio engineering by Walter Sawan. Trailers available on Tel-talk blog.

PAOLA POLETTO

Lady Cleaner

..........Yonge St. / Highway 401

Saw an ad in the supermarket for a lady cleaner, and I liked that the words had been inverted; it reminded me of how I am sometimes an artist and sometimes a coordinator, and constantly switching roles. Here I asked artist Julie Voyce to clean a booth north of Highway 401 on Yonge Street. Julie's voicemail says she is a "cleaner of dirt and maker of things", and it seemed both appropriate and odd to pay her to clean a booth for me for *Tel-talk*.

Photos by Paola Poletto

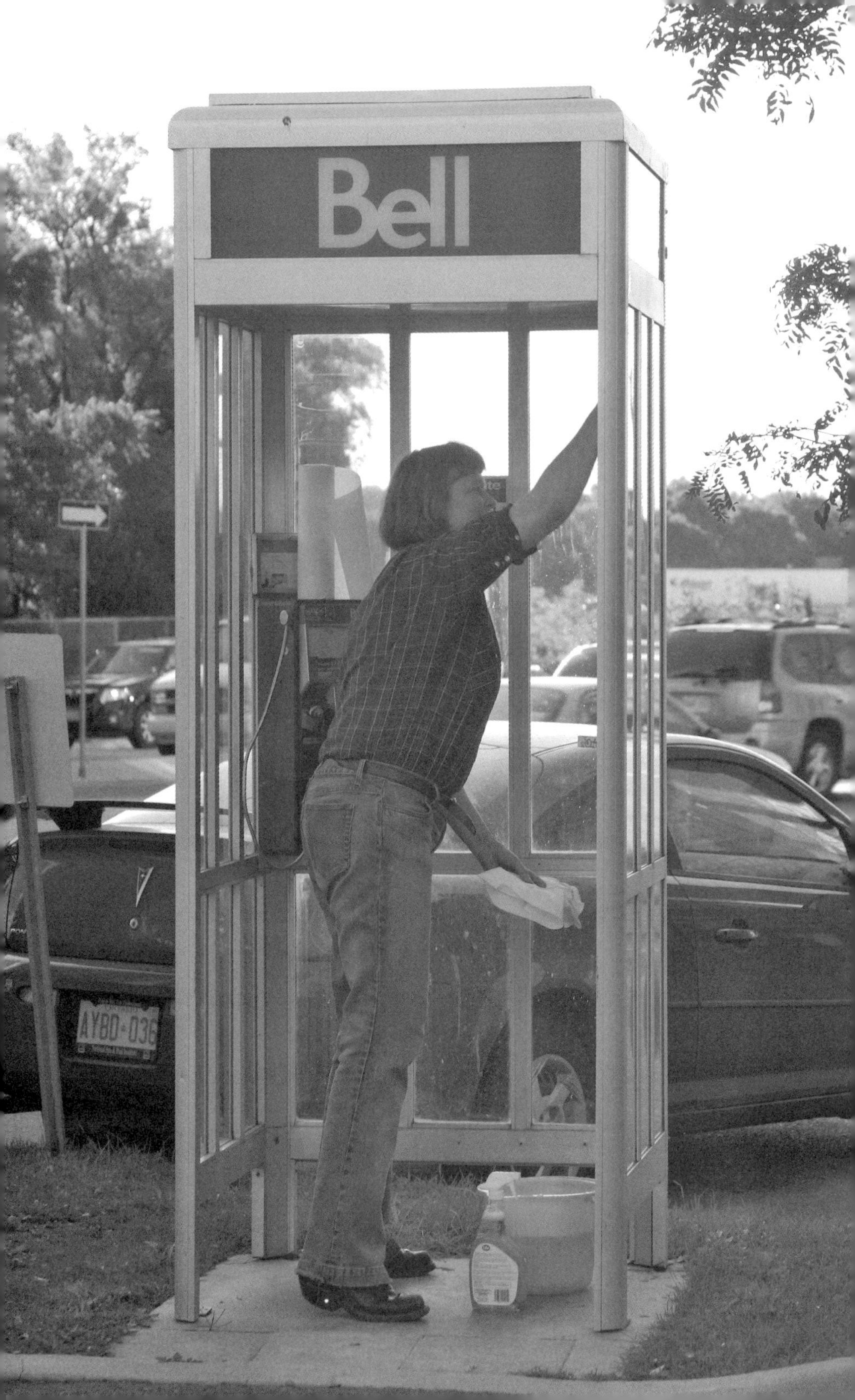
Bell
AYBD-036

PAUL HONG

Telephone

..........*Yonge St. / Churchill Ave.*

Joseph thought he had died but it was apparently only a dream. Later that night, wandering home, he saw a phone booth.

Joseph stepped in to the booth, the doors springing shut behind him. A weak light flickered on and then off. He fished out some coins from his pocket and dropped them into the slot. There was a connection and after a few rings it picked up.

"Hi, you've reached Dial-A-Shrink. How can we help you?"

Joseph took out a sheet of folded foolscap from his pocket and recited the story that he had written while he was at work. When he had finished, he waited.

A high pitched male voice came on: "Forget her. It iz clearly not a match. Move on. It iz never too late to change. There iz a proverb zat's applicable here: no matter how far you've gone down the road, it iz never too late to turn back."

"What?"

"Perhaps ze problem iz zat you are a latent homosexual."

"I'm not."

"How would you know this?"

"I know --"

"Zat is the conundrum the mentally inferior or ze personality zat has so deeply repressed and rationalized zer life zat it is no longer possible to separate truth from fiction.

Zey literally cannot see past ze --"

"Bullshit," Joseph spat.

A woman's voice interjected, "Insert another $1.25, please."

Joseph balked but did as he was told.

There was a pause. "You are a ridiculous farce."

"What?"

"How can I elaborate on such a succinct and self-evident azsessment? Surely you can sense or intuit how fucked up your thought proceszes are? Be honest for once."

"I thought I was."

"You have friendz?"

"Of course."

"But ze number is diminishing, yes?"

"I don't -- why is that happening?"

"Is zit not obvious? Have you not abandoned zem yourself? Have you not only used your friends for your benefit and under your selfish concerns?

"Cursing and gnashing your teeth iz of no use. You must ask yourself what am I doing? What are ze choices zat I am making on a day to day basis zat feeds zis destructive spiral of regret and self-loathing?"

"What the hell," Joseph mumbled. "What do you know, anyhow? You're not even real."

"I am a sophisticated programmable electronic computer designed with ze teachings of ze greatest minds in psychotherapy and sociology. I would say that I am uniquely qualified to understand the noose you have --"

There was a click.

Joseph sighed.

"Your time is up," a woman's voice said.

A couple of days later, unable to sleep Joseph went out for a walk and found himself standing in front of the booth.

He pushed his way inside, picked up the receiver and inserted several coins before stopping. After a moment, he finished dialing. There was a single ring, a click and a series of beeps. "I need some help," Joe pleaded. "Help me."

"Hold your horses… let's take it one step at a time, buckaroo. Okay, now take a deep breath and tell me your story."

It was another electronic computer… another voice simulation. To Joe it sounded like Clint Eastwood or maybe John Wayne.

"I'm going to be laid off, I'm alone, my ex-wife is getting married and I want to end it all."

"I would advise against that course of action. May I suggest you go to a bar, get a stiff drink and think it over?"

"That's your advice?"

"There's a bar across the street from you now. They serve a full range of alcoholic drinks."

"What?"

"Insert another dollar, please."

"Already?"

"Yes."

Joe fished another one from his pocket and inserted it into the slot. "There, now tell me something that I can use."

"Get a gun preferably in pewter with a nice wood finish on the grip. File off the serial number. Then wait until you get your girlfriend --"

"Wife," Joseph interjected, "ex-wife."

"Whatever… get her and her new beau alone and shoot the man first. The order is important the interloper first. Then tell your ex-wife this -- are you writing this down?"

"No, I don't have a pen."

"How's your short term memory?"

"It's okay."

"Never mind, just remember this carefully. Train the pistol on her and scream in a hoarse and hoary manner: 'You did this! You're responsible for all this!' Then, here's the kicker, turn the gun on yourself."

"Wait, what?"

"Shoot yourself in the head. It'd be best through the temple and not the mouth. If you think the going's hard now try surviving a gun shot through the mouth."

"That's your expert advice? And how is any of this funny?"

"Hey, calm down buckaroo."

"Listen here, you lousy --"

There was a click and a buzzing noise. An operator cut in:

"Sir, on behalf of the National Phone Company and Dial-A-Services Incorporated, I am excited to inform you that you are our one millionth caller from this phone booth! Congratulations sir, you've just won a fabulous prize!"

Joseph said nothing.

"Hello?"

"Is this a joke?"

"This is most certainly not a joke, sir. We have been holding a special contest where the millionth caller of a randomly chosen phone booth is awarded a prize of a lifetime and I'm happy to say that special winner is you! Congratulations again and I am certain that this will change your life for the better. Sir, are you excited? How do you feel?"

Joseph hesitated for a moment. "I didn't even know there was a contest... what do I win?"

"Sir, to qualify for your wonderful prize please insert

twenty-five cents now. This tiny charge covers our costs and opens up an opportunity of a lifetime for you --"

"What is this? Is this some sort of scam?"

"Not at all, sir! This is as real as life. You along with several other winners all over our great country are taking part in one of the most exciting contests ever held. Please insert another quarter and prepare yourself for an opportunity of a lifetime!"

Joe glanced down at the quarter in his hand and fed it into the machine.

A marching tune blared out from the receiver. There were also sounds of gunfire or something. Joe held it away from his ear. Over the music, he could barely make out someone talking.

"What? I can't hear you... it's --"

The phone booth shook. Joe thought it was thunder but then the booth began shaking violently and with a whir of machinery it started to descend into the ground with Joe in it.

A few minutes later the light in the booth flickered on and he realized the booth had stopped in a large wood paneled room. There was an oval table in the centre with several chairs. A couple of them were occupied. Hung against the wall behind them, above a set of double doors, was a banner with ribbons. It read, 'Congratulations Joseph Bucket!' in bold hand printed letters.

Joe realized he was still holding the receiver. He replaced it and stepped out slowly. A rat, streaked with dirt, suddenly appeared from behind him and scurried across the room to the double doors. He followed it to the table where his mother was seated.

"Joseph, why am I here?" she asked, looking up at him.

Joseph hugged her and answered, "I won a contest."

He looked over at his friend from grade seven who was now standing. He hadn't changed at all.

"Why are you here?" Joseph asked.

"To celebrate," he said, "obviously."

Joseph noticed a small stack of paper plates, plastic forks and paper napkins in the centre of the table. He counted three of each.

"I guess there aren't any more guests?" he asked. "Is my wife --"

His old friend shook his head.

Joseph looked down at his mother.

"Is that what the cake was for? They took it away but promised they would bring it back," she said, looking at the closed doors. She turned slowly to look up at him. "We were about to have dinner, Joseph, and they brought me here."

"Okay, I'm sure we'll be eating soon."

"You're not married to her anymore, are you?"

"What?"

"You're not married to that girl anymore."

"No."

"That's too bad. I liked her but she was too good for you, Joseph. That's the truth."

Joseph said nothing.

His mother nodded slowly. "Do you think they are going to bring the cake back?"

RYAN BIGGE

Four Short Calls

ring

The payphone is a transformation machine. A place where plots hinge easily, like the doors of the booth itself. A node of danger, possibility and contingency. The hapless protagonist of Paul Hong's story "Telephone" is not only mentally transformed but physically transported through his payphone experience. Regardless of circumstance, everyone ends their call a slightly different person.

ring

The payphone is seedy, tainted by illegalities. The communication method of last resort for those who cannot afford a cellphone – or cannot afford to let certain things escape into the wireless ether. Tethered to a metallic cord, forced to negotiate a filthy mouthpiece, the characters in Cathi Bond's story wait desperately in Cherry Beach for their man to provide chemical freedom. Liz Worth's poem "Aspirations" provides the flipside scenario, with the payphone serving as a post-party confessional for overindulgence.

ring

The payphone is urban. An unofficial landmark indicating significant intersections and marking off distances like a bus stop. Covered in graffiti, gouged with scratches, the payphone absorbs the daily frustrations of city life. Both designed for random encounters, downtown hotels and payphones are a perfect match, as Barry Callaghan's "Déjà vu" demonstrates.

ring

The payphone is disappearing. Gentrified by cellphones, they are now nearly invisible. Hal Niedzviecki's story "Ossington and Dundas" summarizes the reasons for the payphone's eradication – unscrupulous, unhygienic, anonymous. Only in its absence will we realize what has been lost. In the meantime, Jessica Westhead's story "We Understand Each Other on a Cellular Level," offers the future of talk, with its curse and blessing of conversation seepage – overheard snippets that we cannot ignore. We can talk anytime, with nearly anyone, but our voices now originate from nowhere in particular.

click

SHARLENE & PAUL RANKIN

The Telephone Booth

..........*3148 Dundas St. W. (The Telephone Booth Gallery)*

Beyond the expected pop cultural references to the telephone booth of the last century, Superman, Dr. Who, Get Smart, personal memories exist. I had the privilege of spending summers away from the city and its communication conveniences. The telephone booth was a vital lifeline. I have vivid memories of rushing my grandparents to the local general store at a pre-arranged time for a call from one of my parents. The telephone booth was a connection with my other life in the city; a connection to deeply moving personal news such as the death of a relative, and to the more mundane topics such as how is the weather.

The telephone booth of my childhood memories was off by itself, located under a pole light. At night, when the door to the booth was closed, the light from above created a unique space that was at once intensely private and public. This is the power of the telephone booth. When you were in the booth, you were at once on display and hidden. The telephone booth creates a liminal space like few spaces can. As any delinquent can attest to, it is in the shadows and fog where the really fun stuff happens. With the modern advent of continuous communications and ubiquitous contact, the telephone booth is perhaps the last place where magic can occur.

In this way, art galleries are similar to telephone booths. When a patron enters a gallery space, he or she is at once having a private experience with the space, and is also most definitely on display. A successful gallery experience could also be thought of in these terms. Uniquely in the space of a gallery, it is hoped that the tension between the public and the private can allow the patron to experience less of the mundane and more of the deeply moving.

SHEILA BUTLER

Clark Kent and Superman

..........*Dundas St. W. / Bloor St. W.*

In the days when telephone booths existed as small islands of privacy on busy North American streets, Clark Kent, the mild-mannered reporter, often took advantage of this private space to effect the change of clothing that transformed him into Superman, the mighty man-of-steel, the heroic crime fighter. Now, in 2012, many of the phone booths are gone, but the magic transformation of Superman remains vivid in the collective imagination of contemporary culture. Superman's former changing room links the relative disappearance of the phone booth to our changed perceptions of public and personal spaces. *Tel-talk* provides me with the aesthetic opportunity to stage the transformational coming and going of the ongoing legend of Clark Kent and Superman in a now transformed social context.

Photo by Jesse Boles

The Crossways
CYBERWAYS
INTERNET CAFE
416 - 539 - 9393
KIKKAWA COLLEGE
Massage Therapy &
Holistic Therapy
Education
416-762-4857
Public Teaching Clinic
CROSSWAYS ADULT AND YOUTH
JOB CENTRE
Bell
Bell

APPLAUSE
Wellesley St E
155
Bell
PETRO-CANADA
Superphones
with over 25 live
TV channels.
Bell

STUART KEELER

Flagpole (a meta-conversation)

..........Jarvis St. / Wellesley St. E.

Flag and photo credits:

Top: Tiranga (Flag of India) by Avantika; photo by Stuart Keeler

Opposite: Applause and photo by Francis LeBouthillier

The two telephone booths have a piece of metal coming from the top. It looks like a flag pole. So, this is my piece. I put out a call for flags. The flags were posted on the "pole" weekly. People could make the flag, choose to acknowledge their national pride, interpret the notion of what a "flag" is Top- and ultimately fly their own politic.

Your Flag is requested for flying !…
The flag can be a political allegiance, national pride or a conceptual address on the meaning of flags, or you are welcome to interpret the platform with a personal flag of your own design and meaning. The goal of the project is not to censor the flag – rather to present the icon with respect and provide conversation on national or personal identity. The flag can be an existing flag, a hand made flag, a purchased flag, a personal interpretation of a flag. The "flag" is up to you as the participant to decide. The goal is to create dialogue at the corner of the intersection with the mark of private intention within public space.

(Excerpt from call for submissions)

WESEE INC.

Funbooth

..........Christie St. / Lambertlodge Ave.

Phone booths were once novelties and quickly became an assumptive necessity. The advent of the cellular phone and its ensuing popularity relegated the booths to redundancy. The concept of Fun Booth was to transform a vandalized and ignored relic into something appealing. Fun fur and mirrored Mylar were used to create a transient carnivalesque aesthetic. Now a miniature House of Mirrors, the booth reflects the irony of becoming a novelty prop for cell phone snapshots.

Photos by WeeSee Inc.

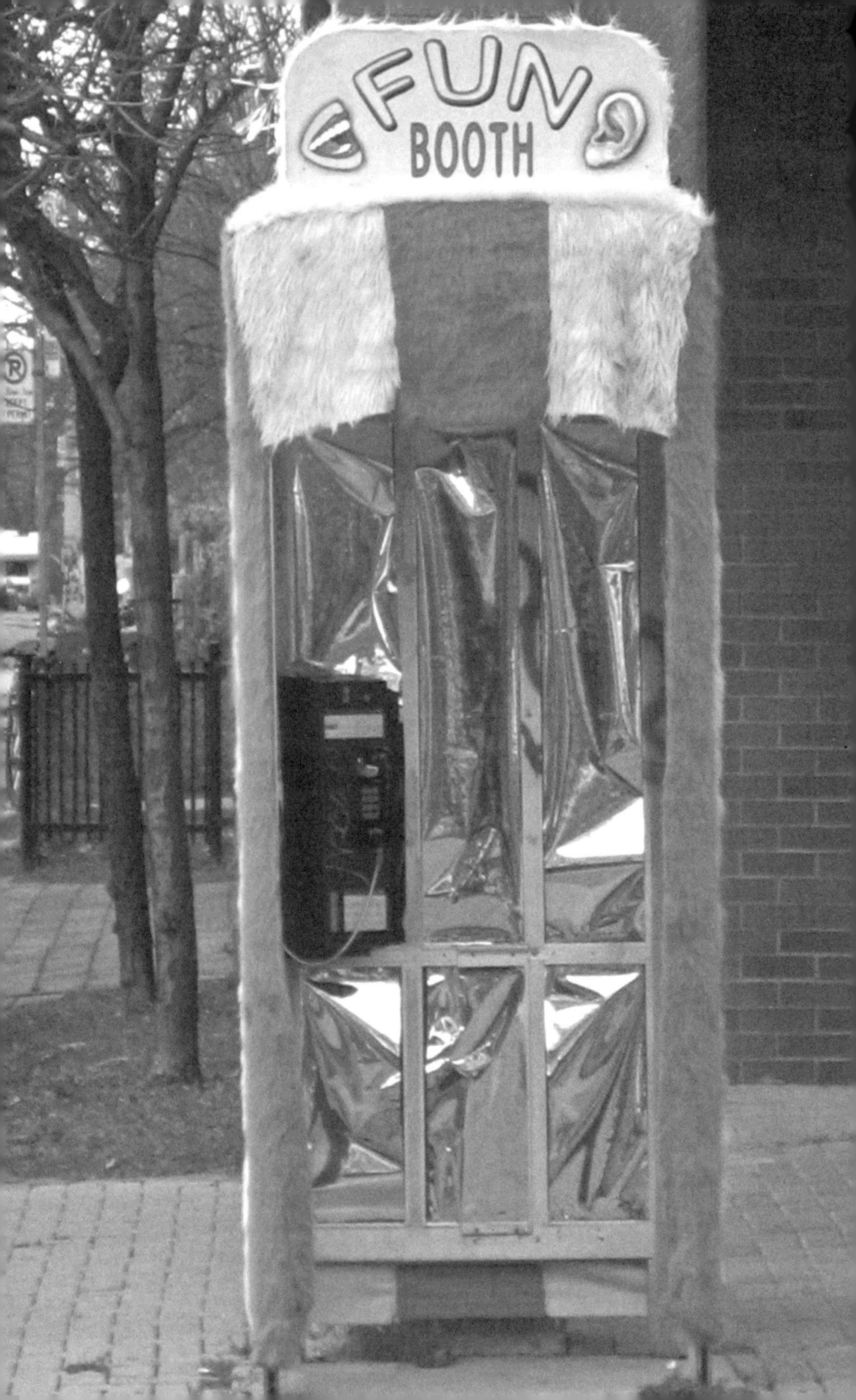
FUN
BOOTH

Tel-talk blog

These and other forthcoming interventions are documented online at www.tel-talk.blogspot.com:

Jamison Food Mart
Alison Fleming
498 Jamison Avenue (Winnipeg, MB)

Pop-Up Memory Shop
During Nuit Blanche London
Charity Miskelly
Dundas Street, between Richmond Street and Clarence Street (London, ON)

Occupy Dundas West
Don McLeod
Telephone Booth Gallery (Toronto, ON)

Lansdowne Light Box
Dyan Marie
Dupont Street and Lansdowne Avenue (Toronto, ON)
(Nearby Coffee Time)

Pickled Egg Poetry Booth
During Artspark
John Sobol
Armstrong Street and Parkdale Avenue (Ottawa, ON)
(Across from the Carleton Tavern)

Away From Home
Laura Peturson
Telephone Booth Gallery

tin can telephone
Lizz Aston
Telephone Booth Gallery

Yesterday, Today, Tomorrow
Maureen Lynett
Exhibition Place (Toronto, ON)

Cellular Ghosts
Steven Tippin
Telephone Booth Gallery

Under the Weather
Tara Cooper and Terry O'Neill
Toronto Island

cell
Jake Kennedy and kevin mcpherson eckhoff
3308 48 Avenue (Vernon, BC)
(At the highway truck stop)

Transformation Booth
TIMEANDDESIRE
Spadina Avenue and College Street (Toronto, ON)
(Spadina Crescent Circle)

AFTERWORD
Paola Poletto

Tel-talk | Medium-message

Every *Tel-talk* intervention is empowered by a specific public context, frequently chosen by a personal memory, or the telephone booth's proximity to the artist's home or place of work. It is also metaphorically wired to a public phone owned by a large corporation. The tensions between public and private space was top-of-mind, as we first started musing and messing about a project that could occupy the streets. Though it was a quick and resolute decision to *not* ask Bell for permission to install art in telephone booths, we also felt a great moral obligation to *not* permanently deface the booth and to hold all artists accountable to this as best we could.

Much of our decision-making was made on the fly and more clearly defined over a breakfast meeting between Sheila Butler, Sharon Switzer, Julie Voyce, Liis Toliao and I. They encouraged us to put something on paper that artists subsequently signed off on; that gave the artists something tangible to show should they be met with any resistance; that set out a buddy system so no one was doing it alone; and that told us when and where something was going up and when it was coming down. No physical residue apart from a peel on-peel off sticker tag revealing the *Tel-talk* blog, www.tel-talk.blogspot.com.

To large effect, the artists who have generously played

along with us were already inclined to work in public spaces, and the authors selected had very characteristic street-savvy literature. All were totally down with smart guerilla tactics. In *The Enabling City*, an online toolkit created by Chiara Camponeschi that espouses upon art interventions that often lead to policy modifications or small changes in the way cities are run, *Tel-talk* might fall within the interventionist forms of "pop-up democracy" taking place in many cities:

> *A shift from control to enablement turns cities into platforms for community empowerment — holistic, living spaces where people make their voices heard and draw from their everyday experiences to affect change.* [2]

Perhaps our greatest and most modest collective goal with *Tel-talk* is to affect change in the way we perceive the telephone booth in our neighbourhoods. Indeed, a dirty relic with a dubious purpose can be viewed as an opportunity to communicate new ideas about place-making; and where art and literature can offer moments of tenderness and care.

Place-making | Make-believe

Anthea Foyer and Rob King's **We Need To Talk** elucidated the great economic and social differences represented in the gold encrusted buildings and art deco friezes of Toronto's financial district and the muddied up headquarters of the 2011 Occupy Toronto Movement, located nearby Queen and Jarvis at St. James Park.

The Bay Street phone sitting in front of Cloud Garden

[2] www.enablingcity.com/about, April 4, 2012.

is pedestal style, centrally positioned and opening up to a wonder wielding view of one of the most elaborate parkettes in Toronto. Most of the people who use the parkette however, are bike couriers, with street uniforms; the antithesis of Bay Street suits.

With a donation by the Ontario Sod Growers Association and Landscape Ontario, St. James Park underwent a makeover late in 2011 to replace the 11,000 square feet of sod trampled on during Occupy Toronto. In response to the park's rehabilitation, a local resident exclaimed, "It is amazing. This is Christmas."[3]

By bringing together these two distinct areas that have been linked by the Occupy Toronto Movement, Anthea and Rob accentuate the conflict between our preconceived ideas of rich and poor, and the actual realities of the specific sites. At first sight of the photo documentation, for instance, it is difficult to discern what booth is where because both sites have a cultural blurriness about them. Surely, most booths are grimy no matter where they are. Perhaps the complexity of the conversation becomes more palpable if you literally walk from one site to the other…

And whether coyly intentional or by a technology glitch of the moment, when I tried to leave a message at the Cloud Garden phone booth, it didn't work. Perplexed, incensed and finally amused, I realized I couldn't leave a message even if I wanted to.

☎

Barry Callaghan offers us a triptych of short stories evoking film noir, replete with cigarette smoke, liquor, and lipstick. Only the foxy lady has aged, and she is hovering somewhere between the Rex Hotel of decades past and what

[3] Connor, Kevin. *St. James Park gets post-Occupy Toronto makeover.* Toronto Sun, Thursday, December 8, 2011.

exists at Queen West and St. Patrick Streets today. Barry's **Déjà vu** stories are deliberate frames. He is struck by the specifics of a moment, a figure, or a particular place. It is precise. **Déjà vu** *is* the Rex Hotel, the street in front of it and the booths across from it. From the booths, he also takes us inside the bar, and into the complicated, darkly humorous mother-son relationship. Somehow, the parasitic logic of a booth to a central place of interest (a hospital, gas station, or the Rex's rhythm and blues bar) is heightened in Barry's stories though it is never actually used.

Tim Laurin settles on a collage image that allows an excess of interpretation, teeming over with pop culture kitsch, and mocking irony.

Barry working his craft outward in and Tim working inward out: their two opposing ways create a delicate tension in place, time and characters. And the final edition of letterpress broadsheets that Tim offers us has slipped happily into Barry's frames.

☎

Hal Niedzviecki's **Ossington and Dundas** captures a slice of life at a very specific street corner, filled with characteristic minutia. The phone booth becomes a place to witness the infinite romance between Ossington and Dundas Streets. The booth is a phallic instrument of these streets, ready to release curdling sperm at any given moment in the form of businesslike calls for call girls, monologues to a sibling and dialogues between lovers, and we are magically caught in an unyielding cross section, or sticky union of these streets through these characters. Hal uses real-time cues to construct a parallel fiction that permits just enough distancing to comment on the shifty ways in which we communicate with lovers, friends and strangers. And the perilous notion of booth as shelter is brilliantly shattered by the 3 am caller's cold feet… a metaphor for the fictitious non-call to one's sister.

☎

Clark Kent and Superman by Sheila Butler personifies this burst of transformative and (pro)creative energy running through many of the interventions. Clark Kent moves from regular guy on the street to superhero, able to leap tall buildings and fly through the sky. Ecstatic and contagious, this universally known story had an infectious effect on the street. Toronto's busy northeast corner of Dundas and Bloor Street West was the perfect setting to engage with art students and transit users. Many passers-by used their cell phones to take photos of/with Superman. Sheila's slightly larger than human scale cut outs were kitschy, replete with an actual tie for Clark, and a brilliant red fabric cape for Superman. The trompe l'oeil expressed a dramatic leap out of the booth and off the sidewalk. These elements provided palatable movement as they were frequently swept up in the brisk February wind, and really, the whole installation precariously held from flying away altogether by a few strategically placed elastic cords. People stopped to watch, comment and share ideas. And by evening, cords, paintings and all had gone MIA in Superman style.

☎

Hitoko Okada begins with the idea of a fashion accessory to create something altogether different in the booth structure. By transposing the concept of clothing to art, she brings forward the actual mechanics of providing shelter and warmth. For **Hive**, Hitoko transformed a pedestal booth into a beehive by adding a booth size beret to the top. A real hive is an enclosed structure where honeybees live and raise their young. The beehive's internal structure is a densely packed matrix of hexagonal cells made of beeswax, called a honeycomb. The bees use the cells to store food (honey and pollen) and to house the "brood" (eggs, larvae, and pupae)… Hey honey, I'm home, he says from **Hive**, the pedestal style booth sporting the biggest, most fashionable art beret/condom in Hamilton. Hitoko caps off the booth and thereby makes visible the absent payphone box.

Lady Toronto | la città

Cathi Bond's **Night Town** trek through Toronto in the 1970's evokes an odd and fresh nostalgia for a sin city, past. The main character, Maddy, is entrenched in a dark dingy place, both physically and emotionally. Through her eyes, we see a Toronto beyond the luring lights and flashy neon lifestyles that a big, get-away city promised her. She is young and worn down by it.

We also sense the dependence on the booth in this particular journey across town; the booths are sites in and of themselves; one could imagine meeting at a booth at so and so, and mapping out a course. Almost always used in solitary, the booths offer little untraceable connections to "home" or "highs". It's a lonely and troubling trip along the way that she creates.

☎

Liz Worth's **Aspirations** is also about girls in the big city: the sexual tensions of the city are embodied in suburban girls out for a night. Liz offers us a contemporary city context for her poem, which is strangely unspecific about place. Not unlike a pastoral poem, she evokes the rural, or in this case, suburban life. However, she transfers the sense of idealism away from the country/suburbs, smacks it into the city in a shocking and refreshing way.

☎

I bequest Liis Toliao the title of "Lady Toronto" for her nine-month-long race through the city documenting any booth she could locate. We started *Tel-talk* with an idea to take photos and make art. Liis has captured busy intersections, remote park corners, derelict industrial zones; green booths, black booths, silver and blue booths. She has enlivened the *Tel-talk* blog, our stories and this book. And there's an editorial film eye to all these cutaways and stop-motion assemblages, over time and a multitude of specific places… like, it's hard to convey a good car chase on the big screen; and it's just as hard to drive around and capture all the really good neighbourhood telephone check points, in artistic photographs, you know? A futile exercise? Liis has gone back to some, and they've disappeared; they've been cleaned up, or tagged, fixed, or broke. Her narrative is noble and it's also what makes it such a rush: to capture a specific banality: the readily accessible and fleeting telephone booth inventory of this lovely city.

☎

There was a rather mature Polish lady who owned "Lady Toronto", a clothing store in upper Roncesvalles Village that I frequently shopped at a few years ago. Her hilarious sales pitch was to pass vintage '80s "Made in Canada" dresses off as if they were runway new. I have a photo of my mother walking along St. Clair Avenue West in 1970, our first year in Canada, and she is wearing a sleek velvet green dress, fresh white flower corsage at her breast, and a pouf hairstyle. Julie Voyce, I love her jeans and plaid shirt style! They own it. These are my Lady Toronto / Lady Cleaner ladies.

Phone Therapy | art therapy

Cleen's **Pay Phone Therapy** was staged in all its melodrama at a booth across from the Mod Club Theatre (more commonly known as the Mod Club). The hand sanitizer and tissues were substantial props for transforming the telephone booth into a minimalist stage for recorded scripts offering therapy. Callers were prompted to become the actor in situ:

Cleen undermines the simple telephone call. Our presumptions about the person on the other end of the line are compromised, and this fake rail welcomes a whole new set of latent possibilities.

☎

Set at College Street and University Avenue, on the edge of the University of Toronto campus, **We Understand Each Other on a Cellular Level: Overheard random**

cellphone monologues as slightly less random dialogue(s) by Jessica Westhead exposes the humour present in the excessive telephone dribble that gets most of us through our day. Assembled together, there is a cathartic quality to the misplaced clichés, the uneven metaphors and the weak ironies and expletives. It connects us to these strangers in a perversely intimate and relatable way.

☎

Julie Voyce's romantic inclinations and cheap aesthetics seemed to fly in the face of Valentine's Day commercialism and get at something closer to the miserable heart and its empty bottles. Through the whole month of February, the fascinators were cared for and their dis/appearances documented by Julie for **Flower Arrangements**. She placed the fascinators in pairs at the lone telephone booths located across the street from a liquor store. Two fascinators begged for company; 10 fascinators made it a month-long party.

☎

Otino Corsano is the writer and director of three "break-up" calls that take place at a booth aptly located in the north end of Toronto, at Finch and Bayview. For **Last Call**, he assumes the industry practices used for a radio spot to predicate his production techniques: locating professional actors and farming out the calls to a sound technician to mix. The fleeting intimacy of the relationship is thus commercialized. It becomes mechanical and impersonal and offers a unique form of denial and numbness.

☎

From booth to mobile to transporter, Paul Hong's **Telephone** offers an idiosyncratic viewpoint of the rapid shift in communication technology. His wild-west, robotic-voiced, reluctant hero messenger, takes us out of time; this story is neither of the past, or the future; it is a parallel dystopia filled with cake and money (cake and money are bad, right?). It is also not a way out: the literal booth tripping, rather, offers psychic complexity. It compels "Joe" to consider all sides of the proverbial payphone coin, and retains us for some serious, or not so serious, introspecting.

☎

For their gutsy **Gallery** gesture, Hayley Isaacs and Hai Ho considered the greatest gift for the telephone booth: to transform it into art. By transposing the stayed signs of a gallery (didactic panel, white walls) to the street, the art object remains in situ. It's a gentle shift: the art object is not redefined by its transposition within the white cube. Rather, the cube takes to the street and gives the telephone booth a great new presence. It is a call to action. Gallery is the new urinal (the telephone booth is the new urinal)!

Broken Telephone | Party Line

WeSee's **Fun Booth** invoked the carnevalesque as a means to take back the booth, and restore it from derelict street furniture to a purposeful object. The purpose: humour and chaos, and to give an indiscriminate street a fresh burst of colour, affecting cell phone snapshots and idle conversations… a neighbourhood nexus. Passerby Derek Flack remarked at the time:

> *I have no idea who put this little intervention together or if there are others around, but in the 10 minutes or so that I spent while taking photos of it, not one person walking by could resist taking a closer look at this strange creation. Not surprisingly, it also acted as something of a tractor beam for kids.*[4]

Fun Booth was installed independent of, but at the same time that *Tel-talk* got underway. The timing was serendipitous, and we unleashed a series of interventions as *Tel-talk* in cahoots.

☎

Stuart Keeler found the set of booths at Jarvis and Wellington peculiar because they supported a pole between them that led to hydro wires above. Unlike other booths, they made visible the notions of power and transmission. Through a call for submissions coordinated by Keeler, **Flagpole (a meta-conversation)** gave individuals an avenue to wave an idea in the form of a flag. From the national symbol of India - proudly shared by the gas attendants across the street - to a polka dot handkerchief with no apparent political agenda, the series of flags that were waved over a six-week period offered the passerby an opportunity to reflect… kitty corner to the booths are a second pair of pedestal booths, offering a curious master and servant dialogue amongst them… That is, if booths could talk and pedestal phones were truly inferior.

---

[4]Flack, Derek. "DIY funhouse revitalizes Toronto phone booth." http://www.blogto.com/arts/2011/11/diy_funhouse_revitalizes_toronto_phone_booth/. November 21, 2011.

☎

The following interventions are documented at www.tel-talk.blogspot.com.

Every booth is an intersection of interest… Dyan Marie's location notes for **Lansdowne Light Box** provide layers of context and specificity:

> South-west corner Dupont and Lansdowne
> The Standard apartment complex was an American Standard toilet factory until the late 1990s that sat derelict for several years until it was renovated into the current large-scale rental unit.

> South-east corner Dupont and Lansdowne
> Formerly a parkette fashioned from a previous TTC turnaround loop, the site has been a seven-story condo building since the early 2000s.

> North-west corner Dupont and Lansdowne
> This classic early-20th-century factory structure is now flagged in advertisements announcing plans to sprout a multi-storey high-rise condo tower from its center core.

> North-east corner Dupont and Lansdowne
> Just north of the telephone booths, 1011 Lansdowne is an infamous rental high-rise known as one of Toronto's 10 worst buildings in press stories that have reported its various transgressions and tragedies. In recent months, improvements efforts are underway to stucco the building's exterior.

Charity Miskelly intends to set-up **Pop-Up Memory Shop** during Nuit Blanche in London to explore and ask,

> *Do the spaces we inhabit absorb our conversations? Are telephone booths really time capsules of past exchanges? Are our secrets and memories forever embedded in our environment?*

Her performance-intervention invites visitors to enter the booth to remember, think, and leave their thoughts, memories and secrets behind. **Pickled Egg Poetry Booth** by John Sobol is set during Artspark in Ottawa. The phone booth he has selected is outside the Carleton Tavern a few blocks from his house. He writes,

> *The tavern was founded in 1935 (and looks like it) and there has probably been a phone booth there for decades. Across the street is a farmer's market/park that is even older. It's sort of an ancient pathway/commercial/ community centre, a narrative nexus in food and drink. My concept is to set up in the booth, with a sign out front saying Pickled Egg Poetry Booth, offering both pickled eggs to passersby and poems, including an offer to call people up and tell them a poem over the phone if people want to give me a number to call. I will also write a poem specially about the tavern that I'll recite to people."*

Jake Kennedy and kevin mcpherson eckhoff have field research:

> *What we'd like to do is go to our local mall here and hang out for a half-day at the bank of phones. while there we're going to 1) call Telus (our Bell) and ask them*

a series of phone-booth-related questions; 2) interview shoppers about phone-booths and 3) give out quarters for free phone calls (which we will ask to record)...

For **cell**, the artists occupy a rural booth in Vernon, British Columbia for a day for what will be a controversial installation of voices and people and telecommunication waves. TIMEANDDESIRE is cocooning a telephone booth for **Transformation Booth**. Visitors are invited to consider making social changes in favor of communal practices.

Tara Cooper and Terry O'Neil will continue to chase the weather to Toronto Island for **Under the Weather**. Alison Fleming, Don McLeod, Laura Peturson, Lizz Alton, Maureen Lynett, and Steven Tippin offer their responses to *Tel-talk* at the Telephone Booth Gallery in the form of paintings and sculptures, and to join this compulsion we all share to fix things. To make things better, cleaner, happier even. And as a means to bring us all together face-to-face, Yvonne Koscielak's intervention comes by way of orchestrating the *Tel-talk* party at the Telephone Booth Gallery!

Steven Tippin's **Cellular Ghosts** are beautiful casts of antiquated cell phones. Nokia, Motorola, LG, Blackberry. He describes how the idea to cast the cast-offs came to him:

> *The glass cell phones were inspired by the culture of the cell phone in two ways. Many years ago before cell phones were as popular as they are now, I lived in Vancouver for a few months. While there I noticed that in every restaurant people would put their cell phones on the right side of their plate so that they could still see*

it while they ate, had conversations or just sat in quiet reflection. I noticed that the phones became almost part of the table settings, in front of every guest, right there beside the spoon. I felt out of place, as I did not have a cell phone. I made up stories in my mind of how I was a second-class citizen or that I did not call ahead to have the restaurant put a cell phone on the table when they placed the silverware, etc. The other reason for the cast cell phones is that technology moves so fast that it becomes obsolete and discarded. That is why the phones are cast out of clear glass to give an ethereal feel to them. They are there and take up the space but not in their full form.

These are the ghosts of old technology, the very same way that booths are ghosts of public service and decorum. Perhaps *technology* is truly one and the same, and we are what changes most. Perhaps one day soon, we will…

Steven Tippin, Cellular Ghosts

Biographies

Alison Fleming was raised mostly in Winnipeg. She briefly studied drawing in Italy and spent a few years working in Europe while developing her painting skills. After returning to Canada, she taught art and English for five years, studied conservation and dedicated more time to painting. She lives in Montreal, where she works as a decorative arts restorer, and is currently painting a series of pictures of Ontario buildings and interiors.

Anthea Foyer (antheafoyer.com) is a diginista, who makes beautiful things using technology, compelling narratives across platforms, and starts conversations between strangers & friends – on and offline. **Rob King** (addi.tv) is a Toronto based new media artist. He is interested in ludology, visualization, generative systems, play, and designing tools for creativity. Most recently he was the artist in residence at the Sonic Arts Research Center at Queen's University in Belfast, developing live visuals for networked music performance.

Barry Callaghan, the well-known novelist, poet, and man of letters, is included in every major Canadian anthology and his fiction and poetry have been translated into seven languages. His works include *The Hogg Poems and Drawings* (1978), *The Black Queen Stories* (1982), *The Way The Angel Spreads Her Wings* (1989). *When Things Get Worst* (1993), *A Kiss Is Still A Kiss* (1995), *Hogg, The Poems And Drawings* (1997), *Barrelhouse Kings: A Memoir* (1998), *Hogg: The Seven Last Words* (2001), *Raise You Five: Essays and Encounters 1964-2004, Volume One* (2005). *Raise You Ten: Essays and Encounters 1964-2004, Volume Two* (2006), *Between Trains* (2007), *Beside Still Waters* (2009), *Raise You Twenty: Essays and Encounters 1964-2011, Volume Three* (2011). He publishes the internationally celebrated quarterly and press, *Exile* and Exile Editions. *Exile* is in its 34th Volume and as editor he has overseen the publication of more than 1000 writers; as for Exile Editions, some 350 titles are in print. **Tim Laurin** studied at Sheridan College School of Design in Mississauga, where he graduated with high honours in 1985. He later studied Fine Arts at Georgian College in Barrie where he continues teaching part time. His work has been exhibited internationally and is included in many collections, most notably the Royal Ontario Museum. In 2009 Tim purchased the historic Tyrone School House in Innisfil, Ontario where he operates Octopus Studio Press.

Cathi Bond is a Canadian writer, broadcaster and novice farmer who freelances for the CBC, rabble and other online media. She's currently working on an adaptation of her first novel, Night Town, which has been formally optioned by Back Alley Films.

Cathi's next project is a prequel to Night Town, a story about two warring families that spans the period between The Great Depression and the end of World War II.

Multidisciplinary artist, **Charity Miskelly**, takes her inspiration from humanity's imprint upon existence. Her work belongs to many private collections, and has been shown in juried, solo and group exhibitions throughout Ontario and abroad. Charity was selected by the City of London to produce a piece of public art in 2011, and has received grants from the Ontario Arts Council. Charity graduated from Western University with a Bachelor of Fine Arts Degree and a Post-Degree Diploma in Arts Management.

Cleen (Colleen Osborn) graduated from the University of Guelph with a BA in Fine Arts and moved to Toronto in 2001 to live like a rock star - if rock stars worked in an office all day. Her first play, *Seen This One Before*, was chosen for the 2006 New Ideas Festival and produced again by The Village Players later that same year. She proudly took part in the 2007 Hysteria Festival with a sculpture installation; images of vibrators and hysteria treatments were projected from the crotch of a female lower torso. Back to theatre, her produced works include *Here to Stay*, showcased as part of the 2008 New Ideas Festival, *The Fecal Monologues* as part of 2009 Toronto Fringe Festival and co-authored *Guantanamo - Hotels and Resorts* performed at Bread & Circus in 2009. She is currently working on a new show *May Contain Milk* to appear in 2012.

Don McLeod is a Toronto based artist. He began exhibiting in 1980 in Owen Sound, throughout the 80s at Toronto's K. Griffin Gallery and most recently at Toronto's Prime Gallery. Don also worked for many years in film industry special effects. He has explored many mediums including steel, wood and fibre-glass. Don's work can be found in corporate and private collections in Canada, United States, France and Qatar.

Dyan Marie is a visual artist exhibiting since 1980. She also responds to urban situations with community initiatives including publications, banner projects, public art, walking systems, festivals and poetry. A founder of *C Magazine*, Cold City Gallery, *Walk Here*, DIG IN, BIG: Bloor Improvement Group, *Bloor Magazine* and *In Public*, Dyan received the City Soul award from the Canadian Urban Institute and various art and community awards from city, provincial and federal government.

Hal Niedzviecki is a writer, speaker, culture commentator and editor whose work challenges preconceptions and confronts readers with the offenses of everyday life. He is the author of eight books including the collection of short stories *Look Down, This is Where it Must Have Happened* (City Lights, April 2011) and the nonfiction book *The Peep Diaries: How We're Learning to Love Watching Ourselves and Our Neighbors* (City Lights, 2009). *The Peep Diaries* was made into a television documentary entitled *Peep Culture* produced for the CBC. He is the current fiction editor and the founder of *Broken Pencil*, the magazine of zine culture and the independent arts (www.brokenpencil.com). He edited the magazine from 1995 to 2002. Hal's writing has appeared in newspapers, periodicals and journals across the world including the *New York Times Magazine, Playboy, the Utne Reader, the Globe and Mail, the National Post, Toronto Life, Walrus, Geist,* and *This Magazine.*

Hayley Isaacs is a visual artist and architectural designer currently working in art direction for film and television. Hayley graduated with her Masters of Architecture from the University of Waterloo in 2007 and has worked at several architectural practices in Vancouver, New York and London. Recently Hayley held the role of Senior Associate at Philip Beesley Architect Inc. in Toronto, designing and comprehensively managing the production and installation of complex, large scale, interactive environments for cultural institutions in Canada, the United States and abroad including *Hylozoic Ground*, Canada's entry to the 2010 Venice Biennale in Architecture. **Hai Ho** is an urban and architectural designer at Sweeny Sterling Finlayson &Co Architects. Most recently, Hai has been involved in several high profile projects for the City of Toronto, including the Lawrence Heights Revitalization Plan, the TTC Waterfront West LRT Feasibility study, the Canadian Tire Head Office, and One York – office, retail, and residential development. Prior to joining &Co in 2007, Hai has worked in architectural practices in Toronto, Vancouver, New York and London, England.

Helena Grdadolnik, principal of Public Workshop, is an architectural activist and public space consultant. She has worked with non-profit organisations, private developers and municipalities in Canada and the UK on developing creative programs and events related to public space. Helena has written for *Canadian Architect, Azure* and *Frame* and has co-authored two books: *Towards an Ethical Architecture* and *The Contemporary Canadian Metropolis*.

Hitoko Okada is a Hamilton-based fashion artist. She holds a Fashion Design Diploma from the International Academy of Design and Technology in Toronto and an Arts and Sciences Diploma from Langara College in Vancouver. She began her career as a props maker and artist with The Public Dreams Society in Vancouver, and has continued to work as a costumer in theater production across Southern Ontario including The Stratford Festival in Stratford, The Grand Theatre in London and Mirvish Productions in Toronto. In 2009, Okada began producing clothing and accessories under the label HITOKOO in which she creates wearable art in small run production. Okada's work has been exhibited in various Toronto venues such as the

Harbourfront Gallery; The Department Gallery and The Gladstone Hotel Gallery; and The Print Studio in Hamilton. Her work is also made available in various retail venues in Southern Ontario and on-line.

kevin mcpherson eckhoff once made an art show with his polished-headed best friend, Jake Kennedy, titled *Words Seen from Gallery Vertigo's Windows: a Community Mural*. It sure was a heckuvalotta fun! He and bff also invent community poetry parties sometimes called "Word Ruckus" and sometimes called "G'morning, Poetry: A Late-Night Humour Talk Show Live!" Send him awkward typos to kevinmcphersoneckhoff atsign geem ale dotic ohm! **Jake Kennedy** is the 4th string co-editor of Gmorningpoetry.blogspot.com and author of the poetrying book *Apollinaire's Speech to the War Medic*. He—with his hirsute best friend of all time, kevin mcpherson eckhoff—is collecting lines for *Death Valley: a Collaborative Community Western* novel. It will be finished soon! Please email hisself at jakedavidkennedy at gee make dot calm—all one word! One love!

Jessica Westhead's fiction has appeared in major literary journals in Canada and the U.S., including *Geist, The New Quarterly,* and *Indiana Review*. Her novel *Pulpy & Midge* was published in 2007 by Coach House Books. Her short story collection *And Also Sharks*, published by Cormorant Books in spring 2011, was a Globe and Mail Top 100 book. She was shortlisted for the 2009 CBC Literary Awards, and one of her stories was selected for the 2011 Journey Prize anthology. She tries to use her cellphone sparingly (and quietly) in public places.

John Sobol is a poet who works at the intersection of oral, literate and digital technologies. He is a passionate improviser and adventurous performer who is as comfortable inventing poems on subways and in supermarkets as he is on stages across Canada and around the world. He has released CDs, written books, run festivals, created residencies, curated exhibitions, produced documentaries and much more. His current work can be found at: www.youareyourmedia.com

Julie Voyce's first exhibtion was a group show: Gallery 76 in 1979 in Toronto. Her most recent exhibition was a group show: *Adventures in Animationland* as part of The 8 fest in 2012 in Toronto. For more details check: www.ccca.ca

Born in Windsor, Ontario, **Laura Peturson** holds a BFA from York University and an MFA from the New York Academy of Art. Laura is represented by Telephone Booth Gallery in Toronto and Darrell Bell Gallery in Saskatoon. With a practice situated in printmaking, drawing and painting, Laura's works combine multiple print-based techniques with a handmade aesthetic. Laura is currently based in Callander, Ontario, and teaches printmaking and painting at Nipissing University.

Liis Toliao burned a Barbie doll in her first short film, which she presented as part of a larger performance piece at the age of 16. She has since been many things including, but not limited to: film editor, construction worker, administrator, fashion merchandiser, photographer, Sunday driver, graphic designer, fairweather optimist and occasional daydreamer. *Tel-talk* represents her first foray into curation and programming. When speaking about *Tel-talk* she says: "I'm interested in finding the awe and wonder in simple moments and common-place objects. Through this project, I hope people re-discover the telephone booth. They're beautiful spaces."

Liz Worth is the Toronto-based author of *Amphetamine Heart* (Guernica Editions, 2011), *Treat Me Like Dirt: An Oral History of Punk in Toronto and Beyond 1977-1981* (Bongo Beat/ECW, 2011) and *Eleven: Eleven* (Trainwreck Press, 2008), a shot of surreal punk fiction.

Lizz Aston is a graduate of the Textiles program at the School of Crafts and Design, Sheridan College and has recently completed an artist-in-residence program in the Craft Department at Harbourfront Centre. Through her work, she focuses on making concept-based fibre art and sculpture that has been developed with regards to both traditional and contemporary textile processes. Her award winning work was recently included an international textiles exhibition, *Love Lace*, at the Powerhouse Museum, Sydney, Australia.

Maureen Lynett is a Toronto based artist. She graduated from the University of Windsor, Bachelor of Arts and continued her studies at Three Schools, Toronto. Her main interest is figurative painting. Since 1984 she has exhibited in both Toronto and New York galleries, most recently at Toronto's Prime Gallery. Her work can be found in corporate and private collections in Canada, United States and the Dominican Republic.

Otino Corsano is a new genre artist conceptually linked to the Los Angeles art scene. His recent work attempts to construct films using other media. Corsano employs the format of the artist interview as an extension of his neo-conceptual practice. His art writings and interviews are published in *artUS magazine* (LA), ARTPOST, Akimblog and his own blog. He has taught at the University of Toronto and is a Sessional Instructor at OCAD University.

Paola Poletto is an artist, writer and arts administrator. She is co-editor of *Boredom Fighters!* (Tightrope Books, 2008), *Ourtopias: Cities and the Role of Design* (Riverside Architectural Press, 2008); and co-founder/editor of *Kiss Machine* (2000-5), which included a girls and guns issue with traveling exhibition to artist run centres in

Eastern Europe. In 2009, Paola was guest curator of *fashion no-no* (Queens Quay Gallery, Harbourfront Centre). She has also held curatorial and programming positions at Toronto's Italian Cultural Institute (1993-98), Design Exchange (2000-2008) and the City of Mississauga's Culture Division (2008-).

Paul Hong's short stories have appeared in *blood & aphorisms, Broken Pencil, Kiss Machine* and various anthologies. He is the author of *Your love is murder or the case of the mangled pie* (Tightrope Books, 2006) and fits nicely into a phone booth.

Ryan Bigge is a digital content strategist, cultural journalist and cocktail enthusiast. His debut novel will be published by Tightrope Books in the Fall of 2013. He is also co-creator of tweet2hold.com and txt2hold.com, two interactive projects that convert ephemeral digital experiences into tangible physical objects.

Sharlene Rankin is a graduate of the Honours Bachelor of Fine Arts Program (Visual Arts, summa cum laude 2001), York University, Toronto. For the past 10 years, she has worked extensively in arts administration. Her unique combination of work experience has provided her with a strong background in Canadian art history and the art scene in Canada. She has served as Executive Director of the Art Dealers Association of Canada (ADAC) and of Headwaters Arts, a regional not-for-profit arts organization and festival. She has also worked in public and commercial art galleries including the Art Gallery of Peel. She is currently the Owner and Director of the Telephone Booth Gallery in Toronto.

Sheila Butler is a visual artist exhibiting in Canada and abroad. Since 1969 Butler has worked with Inuit artists from Baker Lake, Nunavut. Butler taught at the University of Manitoba and the University of Winnipeg, moving to the University of Western Ontario until retirement from teaching in 2004. Butler's work is grounded in representational drawing/painting. Her practice is characterized by solo exhibitions and by collective work with other artists, especially in relation to activist art projects relating to feminist and to aboriginal issues. Butler's work is included in the collections of the National Gallery of Canada, and the University of Toronto, among others.

Steven Tippin is a glass artist living and working in Wellesley, Ontario. He is the Vice President and Ontario representative for the Glass Art Association of Canada. Tippin received his Undergraduate Bachelor degree in Printmaking and Sculpture from the University of Guelph in 2002. He returned to school in 2005 to study at the glass Department of Sheridan College and recently graduated from the Masters of Fine Arts program at the Rochester Institute of Technology.

Stuart Keeler: I see the dysfunctional aesthetics of the built environment a long time friend. I see a fascinating duality of comic and tragic in the spaces of the modern city, with this I want my work to read as an institutionalized poetic collaboration between Jerry Seinfeld and Mies Van Der Rohe. My approach is an investigative research of the (transitional) spaces found in the visual culture of our urban spaces, an ever-expanding behemoth that denies a steadfast floor plan. Recent exhibitions: Yerba Buena Center for the Arts, John Michael Kohler Art Center, The Contemporary. Curatorial projects: LEITMOTIF-Scotiabank Nuit Blanche, Le Flash, Art 44|46. Recent Grants: Ontario Art Council (OAC), Service Works, Rauchenberg Foundation.

As collaborators, **Tara Cooper** and **Terry O'Neill** work across disciplines from printmaking, animation and sound to documentary filmmaking and sculpture. Employing the strategies of creative non-fiction, their research combines fieldwork and footwork. Their most recent study involving the language of weather has led them to embark on a storm chasing tour in Oklahoma. Tara works as an Assistant Professor at The University of Waterloo and Terry works as an art director for the CBC.

TIMEANDDESIRE examines the concept of shared spaces and the role perception plays in constructing our realities. It challenges presumptions that affect our view of the environment, interactions, observations and activities therein. Recent works include Toronto Urban Film Festival 2011, *Prefix Photo Journal* Issue 24 2011, Art of the Danforth 2012 and forthcoming Nuit Blanche, 2012. Denise St Marie established TIMEANDDESIRE from her practice and has recently begun collaborating with Philosopher Timothy Walker on several projects.

WeSee Inc. is the collective moniker under which Roy Kohn and Kate Vasyliw generate collaborative art projects. Kohn and Vasyliw are multidisciplinary artists that have been producing collaborative art projects as WeSee Inc. since 2007. They are co-founders and co-curators of Roadside Attractions, a site-specific art project space. They are based in a storefront studio in Toronto, Canada.

Yvonne Koscielak is an art advisor, cultural worker and creative producer. She received her Master's in Art Business from the Sotheby's Institute – New York, and her HBA from the University of Toronto, and has held curatorial and consulting positions throughout New York and Toronto where her brief included acquisition and de-accession of many notable corporate and private art collections. Yvonne specializes in Modern and Contemporary art and can regularly be found spending the afternoon at a local art gallery or cashing in her travel points to avoid missing the latest art fair or museum exhibition.

Acknowledgements

Immense gratitude to all the writers and artists who took this project on with us and offered guidance and assurances along the way. Thanks to R.M. Vaughan for his article in the Globe and Mail that doubled our total blog visitors in the course of a day. Thanks to Bell and our workday colleagues in Mississauga for staying cool and distant. Thanks to Halli Villegas at Tightrope Books and Sharlene Rankin at the Telephone Booth Gallery for taking a risk on the project. And in the spirit of Okada's *Hive*, thank you to our honeys: Dennis Monestier, David Penteliuk, and Paul, Marinella and Esme Hong.

Paola Poletto thanks the Ontario Arts Council and Tightrope Books for their financial support through the Writer's Reserve Program. She also thanks Liis for starting us on the idea that eagerly led us to *Tel-talk* and its fancy blog, and Yvonne for organizing the art party/launch.

Liis Toliao: Infinite thanks to my accomplices in art - To Yvonne for signing on to this lovely madness before reading the fine print and to Paola for showing me what "running with an idea" really means. Thanks to JoBu for his generous loan of a laptop in a book layout emergency. Thanks to my hype man, Dave, for his encouragement and for being at the ready for every payphone adventure. And many thanks to my Dad, who didn't care that I didn't want to be an accountant.

Someone once said "if we discovered we only had five minutes left to say all we wanted to say, every telephone booth would be occupied by people telling other people that they loved them" – it is with this spirit in mind that Yvonne Koscielak would like to thank all of the contributors, friends and loved ones whose enthusiasm and support was responsible for the success of *Tel-talk*. Also, a very special thank you to Liis and Paola for their daily dose of inspiration and creative genius.

Déjà vu (1) by Barry Callaghan was published in *Between Trains,* McArthur and Company, Toronto, 2007.